Ed McBain

DOLL

"ONE OF THE MOST FEROCIOUS CASES THAT MR. McBAIN HAS YET DUG UP...AND THERE IS A NAMELESS SEDUCTRESS ON-STAGE WHO IS BEYOND ANY DOUBT HIS MOST CREDIBLE NIGHTMARE CREATION."
New Yorker

"ENGROSSING...ANOTHER EXCELLENT CRIME DETECTION STORY."
Newsday

"SUSPENSE IS ALL THE BETTER...A SPELL OF GORY AND SEXY SCENES DELIVERED AT FIRST HAND."
San Francisco Chronicle

DOLL

AN 87TH PRECINCT NOVEL

Ed McBain

◆ **AVON**
PUBLISHERS OF BARD, CAMELOT, DISCUS AND FLARE BOOKS

AVON BOOKS
A division of
The Hearst Corporation
1790 Broadway
New York, New York 10019

Copyright © 1965 by Ed McBain
Published by arrangement with the author
Library of Congress Catalog Card Number: 85-91260
ISBN: 0-380-70082-4

First Avon Printing, April 1986

AVON TRADEMARK REG. U.S. PAT. OFF. AND IN
OTHER COUNTRIES, MARCA REGISTRADA, HECHO EN
U. S. A.

Printed in the U.S.A.

K-R 10 9 8 7 6 5 4 3 2 1

This, too, is for Dodie and Ray Crane

The city in these pages is imaginary.
The people, the places are all fictitious.
Only the police routine is based on
established investigatory technique.

Chapter One

The child Anna sat on the floor close to the wall and
played with her doll, talking to it, listening. She could
hear the voices raised in anger coming from her mother's bedroom through the thin separating wall, but she
busied herself with the doll and tried not to be frightened. The man in her mother's bedroom was shouting
now. She tried not to hear what he was saying. She
brought the doll close to her face and kissed its plastic
cheek, and then talked to it again, and listened.

In the bedroom next door, her mother was being
murdered.

Her mother was called Tinka, a chic and lacquered
label concocted by blending her given name, Tina, with
her middle name, Karin. Tinka was normally a beautiful
woman, no question about it. She'd have been a beautiful woman even if her name was Beulah. Or Bertha. Or
perhaps even Brunhilde. The Tinka tag only enhanced
her natural good looks, adding an essential gloss, a necessary polish, an air of mystery and adventure.

Tinka Sachs was a fashion model.

She was, no question about it, a very beautiful woman. She possessed a finely sculptured face that was perfectly suited to the demands of her profession, a wide
forehead, high pronounced cheekbones, a generous
mouth, a patrician nose, slanted green eyes flecked with
chips of amber; oh, she was normally a beauty, no question about it. Her body was a model's body, lithe and
loose and gently angled, with long slender legs, narrow
hips, and a tiny bosom. She walked with a model's insin-
uating glide, pelvis tilted, crotch cleaving the air, head
erect. She laughed with a model's merry shower of musi-
cal syllables, painted lips drawing back over capped
teeth, amber eyes glowing. She sat with a model's care-
lessly draped ease, posing even in her own living room,
invariably choosing the wall or sofa that best offset her
clothes, or her long blonde hair, or her mysterious green

1

eyes flecked with chips of amber; oh, she was normally a beauty.

She was not so beautiful at the moment.

She was not so beautiful because the man who followed her around the room shouting obscenities at her, the man who stalked her from wall to wall and boxed her into the narrow passage circumscribed by the king-sized bed and the marble-topped dresser opposite, the man who closed in on her oblivious to her murmuring, her pleading, her sobbing, the man was grasping a kitchen knife with which he had been slashing her repeatedly for the past three minutes.

The obscenities spilled from the man's mouth in a steady unbroken torrent, the anger having reached a pitch that was unvaried now, neither rising nor falling in volume or intensity. The knife blade swung in a short, tight arc, back and forth, its rhythm as unvaried as that of the words that poured from the man's mouth. Obscenities and blade, like partners in an evil copulation, moved together in perfect rhythm and pitch, enveloping Tinka in alternating splashes of blood and spittle. She kept murmuring the man's name pleadingly, again and again, as the blade ripped into her flesh. But the glittering arc was relentless. The razor-sharp blade, the monotonous flow of obscenities, inexorably forced her bleeding and torn into the far corner of the room, where the back of her head collided with an original Chagall, tilting it slightly askew, the knife moving in again in its brief terrifying arc, the blade slicing parallel bleeding ditches across her small breasts and moving lower across the flat abdomen, her peignoir tearing again with a clinging silky blood-sotted sound as the knife blade plunged deeper with each step closer he took. She said his name once more, she shouted his name, and then she murmured the word 'Please', and then she fell back against the wall again, knocking the Chagall from its hook so that a riot of framed color dropped heavily over her shoulder, falling in a lopsided angle past the long blonde hair, and the open red gashes across her throat and naked chest, the tattered blue peignoir, the natural brown of her exposed pubic hair, the blue satin slippers. She fell gasping for breath, spitting blood, headlong over the painting, her forehead colliding with the wide oaken frame, her blonde hair covering the Chagall reds and yellows and violets with a fine misty golden haze, the knife slash across her throat pouring blood onto the canvas, setting her hair afloat in a pool of red that finally overspilled the oaken frame and ran onto the carpet.

Next door, the child Anna clung fiercely to her doll.

She said a reassuring word to it, and then listened in terror as she heard footfalls in the hall outside her closed bedroom door. She kept listeining breathlessly until she heard the front door to the apartment open and then close again.

She was still sitting in the bedroom, clutching her doll, when the superintendent came up the next morning to change a faucet washer Mrs Sachs had complained about the day before.

April is the fourth month of the year.

It is important to know that—if you are a cop, you can sometimes get a little confused.

More often than not, your confusion will be compounded of one part exhaustion, one part tedium, and one part disgust. The exhaustion is an ever-present condition and one to which you have become slowly accustomed over the years. You know that the department does not recognize Saturdays, Sundays, or legal holidays, and so you are even prepared to work on Christmas morning if you have to, especially if someone intent on committing mischief is inconsiderate enough to plan it for that day—witness Gerneral George Washington and the unsuspecting Hessians, those drunks. You know that a detective's work schedule does not revolve around a fixed day, and so you have learned to adjust to your odd waking hours and your shorter sleeping time, but you have never been able to adjust to the nagging feeling of exhaustion that is the result of too much crime and too few hours, too few men to pit against it. You are sometimes a drag at home with your wife and children, but that is only because you are tired, boy what a life, all work and no play, wow.

The tedium is another thing again, but it also helps to generate confusion. Crime is the most exciting sport in the world, right? Sure, ask anybody. Then how come it can be so boring when you're a working cop who is typing reports in triplicate and legging it all over the city talking to old ladies in flowered house dresses in apartments smelling of death? How can the routine of detection become something as prescribed as the ritual of a bullfight, never changing, so that even a gun duel in a nighttime alley can assume familiar dimensions and be regarded with the same feeling of ennui that accompanies a routine request to the B.C.I.? The boredom is confusing as hell. It clasps hands with the exhaustion and makes you wonder whether this is January or Friday.

The disgust comes into it only if you are a human being. Some cops aren't. But if you are a human being, you are sometimes appalled by what your fellow human beings are capable of doing. You can understand lying because you practice it in a watered-down form as a daily method of smoothing the way, helping the machinery of mankind to function more easily without getting fouled by too much truth-stuff. You can understand stealing because when you were a kid you sometimes swiped pencils from the public school supply closet, and once a toy airplane from the five and ten. You can even understand murder because there is a dark and secret place in your own heart where you have hated deeply enough to kill. You can understand all these things, but you are nonetheless disgusted when they are piled upon you in profusion, when you are constantly confronted with liars, thieves and slaughterers, when all human decency seems in a state of suspension for the eight or twelve or thirty-six hours you are in the squadroom or out answering a squeal. Perhaps you could accept an occasional corpse—death is only a part of life, isn't it? It is corpse heaped upon corpse that leads to disgust and further leads to confusion. If you can no longer tell one corpse from another, if you can no longer distinguish one open bleeding head from the next, then how is April any different from October?

It was April.

The torn and lovely woman lay in profile across the bloody face of the Chagall painting. The lab technicians were dusting for latent prints, vacuuming for hairs and traces of fiber, carefully wrapping for transportation the knife found in the corridor just outside the bedroom door, the dead girl's pocket book, which seemed to contain everything but money.

Detective Steve Carella made his notes and then walked out of the room and down the hall to where the little girl sat in a very big chair, her feet not touching the floor, her doll sleeping across her lap. The little girl's name was Anna Sachs—one of the patrolmen had told him that the moment Carella arrived. The doll seemed almost as big as she did.

'Hello,' he said to her, and felt the old confusion once again, the exhaustion because he had not been home since Thursday morning, the tedium because he was embarking on another round of routine questioning, and the disgust because the person he was about to question was only a little girl and her mother was dead and mutilated in the room next door. He tried to smile. He was not very good at it. The little girl said nothing. She looked up at him out of very big eyes. Her lashes were long and brown, her mouth drawn in stoic silence beneath a nose she had inherited from her mother. Unblinkingly, she watched him. Unblinkingly, she said nothing.

'You name is Anna, isn't it?' Carella said.

The child nodded.

'Do you know what my name is?'

'No.'

'Steve.'

The child nodded again.

'I have a little girl about your age,' Carella said. 'She's a twin. How old *are* you, Anna?'

'Five.'

'That's just how old my daughter is.'

'Mmm,' Anna said. She paused a moment, and then asked, 'Is Mommy killed?'

'Yes,' Carella said. 'Yes, honey, she is.'

'I was afraid to go in and look.'

'It's better you didn't.'

'She got killed last night, didn't she?' Anna asked.

'Yes.'

There was a silence in the room. Outside, Carella could hear the muted sounds of a conversation between the police photographer and the m.e. An April fly buzzed against the bedroom window. He looked into the child's upturned face.

'Were you here last night?' he asked.

'Um-huh.'

'Where?'

'Here. Right here in my room.' She stroked the doll's cheek, and then looked up at Carella and asked, 'What's a twin?'

'When two babies are born at the same time.'

'Oh.'

She continued looking up at him, her eyes tearless, wide, and certain in the small white face. At last she said, 'The man did it.'

'What man?' Carella asked.

'The one who was with her.'

'Who?'

'Mommy. The man who was with her in her room.'

'Who was the man?'

'I don't know.'

'Did you see him?'

'No. I was here playing with Chatterbox when he came in.'

'Is Chatterbox a friend of yours?'

'Chatterbox is my *dolly*,' the child said, and she held up the doll and giggled, and Carella wanted to scoop her into his arms, hold her close, tell her there was no such thing as sharpened steel and sudden death.

'When was this, honey?' he asked. 'Do you know what time it was?'

'I don't know,' she said, and shrugged. 'I only know how to tell twelve o'clock and seven o'clock, that's all.'

'Well . . . was it dark?'

'Yes, it was after supper.'

'This man came in after supper, is that right?'

'Yes.'

'Did your mother know this man?'

'Oh, yes,' Anna said. 'She was laughing and everything when he first came in.'

'Then what happened?'

'I don't know.' Anna shrugged again. 'I was here playing.'

There was another silence.

The first tears welled into her eyes suddenly, leaving the rest of the face untouched; there was no trembling of lip, no crumbling of features, the tears simply over-spilled her eyes and ran down her cheeks. She sat as still as a stone, crying soundlessly while Carella stood before her helplessly, a hulking man who suddenly felt weak and ineffective before this silent torrent of grief.

He gave her his handkerchief.

She took it wordlessly and blew her nose, but she did not dry her eyes. Then she handed it back to him and said, 'Thank you,' with the tears still running down her face endlessly, sitting stunned with her small hands fold-ed over the doll's chest.

'He was hitting her,' she said. 'I could hear her crying, but I was afraid to go in. So I . . . I made be-lieve I didn't hear. And then . . . then I *really* didn't hear. I just kept talking with Chatterbox, that was all. That way I couldn't hear what he was doing to her in the other room.'

'All right, honey,' Carella said. He motioned to the patrolman standing in the doorway. When the patrol-man joined him, he whispered, 'Is her father around? Has he been notified?'

'Gee, I don't know,' the patrolman said. He turned and shouted, 'Anybody know if the husband's been con-tacted?'

A Homicide cop standing with one of the lab techni-cians looked up from his notebook and said, 'He's in Arizona. They been divorced for three years now.'

Lieutenant Peter Byrnes was normally a patient and understanding man, but there were times lately when Bert Kling gave him a severe pain in the ass. And whereas Byrnes, being patient and understanding, could appreciate the reasons for Kling's behavior, this in no way made Kling any nicer to have around the office. The way Byrnes figured it, psychology was certainly an important factor in police work because it helped you to recognize that there were no longer any villains in the world, there were only disturbed people. Psychology substituted understanding for condemnation. It was a very nice tool to possess, psychology was, until a cheap thief kicked you in the groin one night. It then become somewhat difficult to imagine the thief as a put-upon soul who'd had a shabby childhood. In much the same way, though Byrnes completely understood the trauma that was responsible for Kling's current behavior, he was finding it more and more difficult to accept Kling as anything but a cop who was going to hell with himself.

'I want to transfer him out,' he told Carella that morning.

'Why?'

'Because he's disrupting the whole damn squadroom, that's why,' Byrnes said. He did not enjoy discussing this, nor would he normally have asked for consultation on any firm decision he had made. His decision, however, was anything but final, that was the damn thing about it. He liked Kling, and yet he no longer liked him. He thought he could be a good cop, but he was turning into a bad one. 'I've got enough bad cops around here,' he said aloud.

'Bert isn't a bad cop,' Carella said. He stood before Byrnes's cluttered desk in the corner office and listened to the sounds of early spring on the street outside the building, and he thought of the five-year-old girl named Anna Sachs who had taken his handkerchief while the tears streamed down her face.

'He's a surly shit,' Byrnes said. 'Okay, I know what happened to him, but people have died before, Steve, people have been killed before. And if you're a man you grow up to it, you don't act as if everybody's responsible for it. We didn't have anything to do with his girl friend's death, that's the plain and simple truth, and I personally am sick and tired of being blamed for it.'

'He's not blaming you for it, Pete. He's not blaming any of us.'

'He's blaming the *world*, and that's worse. This morning, he had a big argument with Meyer just because Meyer picked up the phone on his desk. I mean, the goddamn phone was ringing, so instead of crossing the room to his own desk, Meyer picked up the closest phone, which was on Kling's desk, so Kling starts a row. Now you can't have that kind of attitude in a squadroom where men are working together, you can't have it, Steve. I'm going to ask for his transfer.'

'That'd be the worst thing that could happen to him.'

'It'd be the best thing for the squad.'

'I don't think so.'

'Nobody's asking your advice,' Byrnes said flatly.

'Then why the hell did you call me in here?'

'You see what I mean?' Byrnes said. He rose from his desk abruptly and began pacing the floor near the meshed-grill windows. He was a compact man and he moved with an economy that belied the enormous energy in his powerful body. Short for a detective, muscular, with a bullet-shaped head and small blue eyes set in a face seamed with wrinkles, he paced briskly behind his desk and shouted, 'You see the trouble he's causing? Even you and I can't sit down and have a sensible discussion about him without starting to yell. That's *just* what I mean, that's *just* why I want him out of here.'

'You don't throw away a good watch because it's running a little slow,' Carella said.

'Don't give me any goddamn similes,' Byrnes said. 'I'm running a squadroom here, not a clock shop.'

'Metaphors,' Carella corrected.

'What*ever*,' Byrnes said. 'I'm going to call the Chief tomorrow and ask him to transfer Kling out. That's it.'

'Where?'

'What do you mean *where*? What do I care where? Out of here, that's all.'

'But *where*? To another squadroom with a bunch of strange guys, so he can get on *their* nerves even more than he does ours? So he can—'

'Oh, so you admit it.'

'That Bert gets on my nerves? Sure, he does.'

'And the situation isn't improving, Steve, you know that too. It gets worse every day. Look, what the hell am I wasting my breath for? He goes, and that's it.' Byrnes gave a brief emphatic nod, and then sat heavily in his chair again, glaring up at Carella with an almost childish challenge on his face.

Carella sighed. He had been on duty for close to fifty

hours now, and he was tired. He had checked in at eight-forty-five Thursday morning, and been out all that day gathering information for the backlog of cases that had been piling up all through the month of March. He had caught six hours' sleep on a cot in the locker room that night, and then been called out at seven on Friday morning by the fire department, who suspected arson in a three-alarm blaze they'd answered on the South Side. He had come back to the squadroom at noon to find four telephone messages on his desk. By the time he had returned all the calls—one was from an assistant m.e. who took a full hour to explain the toxicological analysis of a poison they had found in the stomach contents of a beagle, the seventh such dog similarly poisoned in the past week—the clock on the wall read one-thirty. Carella sent down for a pastrami on rye, a container of milk, and a side of French fries. Before the order arrived, he had to leave the squadroom to answer a burglary squeal on North Eleventh. He did not come back until five-thirty, at which time he turned the phone over to a complaining Kling and went down to the locker room to try to sleep again. At eleven o'clock Friday night, the entire squad, working in flying wedges of three detectives to a team, culminated a two-month period of surveillance by raiding twenty-six known numbers banks in the area, a sanitation project that was not finished until five on Saturday morning. At eight-thirty a.m., Carella answered the Sachs squeal and questioned a crying little girl. It was now ten-thirty a.m., and he was tired, and he wanted to go home, and he didn't want to argue in favor of a man who had become everything the lieutenant said he was, he was just too damn weary. But earlier this morning he had looked down at the body of a woman he had not known at all, had seen her ripped and lacerated flesh, and had felt a pain bordering on nausea. Now—weary, bedraggled, unwilling to argue—he could remember the mutilated beauty of Tinka Sachs, and he felt something of what Bert Kling must have known in that Culver Avenue bookshop not four years ago when he'd held the bullet-torn body of Claire Townsend in his arms.

'Let him work with me,' he said.

'What do you mean?'

'On the Sachs case. I've been teaming with Meyer lately. Give me Bert instead.'

'What's the matter, don't you like Meyer?'

'I *love* Meyer, I'm tired, I want to go home to bed, will you please let me have Bert on this case?'

'What'll that accomplish?'

'I don't know.'

'I don't approve of shock therapy,' Byrnes said. 'This Sachs woman was brutally murdered. All you'll do is remind Bert—'

'Therapy, my ass,' Carella said. 'I want to be with him, I want to talk to him, I want to let him know he's still got some people on this goddamn squad who think he's a decent human being worth saving. Now, Pete, I *really* am very very tired and I don't want to argue this any further, I mean it. If you want to send Bert to another squad, that's your business, you're the boss here, I'm not going to argue with you, that's all. I mean it. Now just make up your mind, okay?'

'Take him,' Byrnes said.

'Thank you,' Carella answered. He went to the door. 'Good night,' he said, and walked out.

Chapter Two

Sometimes a case starts like sevens coming out.

The Sachs case started just that way on Monday morning when Steve Carella and Bert Kling arrived at the apartment building on Stafford Place to question the elevator operator.

The elevator operator was close to seventy years old, but he was still in remarkable good health, standing straight and tall, almost as tall as Carella and of the same general build. He had only one eye, however—he was called Cyclops by the superintendent of the building and by just about everyone else he knew—and it was this single fact that seemed to make him a somewhat less than reliable witness. He had lost his eye, he explained,

in World War I. It had been bayoneted out of his head
by an advancing German in the Ardennes Forest. Cyclops—who up to that time had been called Ernest—
had backed away from the blade before it had a chance
to pass completely through his eye and into his brain,
and then had carefully and passionlessly shot the German three times in the chest, killing him. He did not realize his eye was gone until he got back to the aid station. Until then, he thought the bayonet had only
gashed his brow and caused a flow of blood that made it
difficult to see. He was proud of his missing eye, and
proud of the nickname Cyclops. Cyclops had been a
giant, and although Ernest Messner was only six feet
tall, he had lost his eye for democracy, which is as good
a cause as any for which to lose an eye. He was also
very proud of his remaining eye, which he claimed was
capable of twenty/twenty vision. His remaining eye was
a clear penetrating blue, as sharp as the mind lurking
somewhere behind it. He listened intelligently to everything the two detectives asked him, and then he said,
'Sure, I took him up myself.'

'You took a man up to Mrs Sachs's apartment Friday
night?' Carella asked.

'That's right.'

'What time was this?'

Cyclops thought for a moment. He wore a black
patch over his empty socket, and he might have looked
a little like an aging Hathaway Shirt man in an elevator
uniform, except that he was bald. 'Must have been nine
or nine-thirty, around then.'

'Did you take the man *down,* too?'

'Nope.'

'What time did you go off?'

'I didn't leave the building until eight o'clock in the
morning.'

'You work from when to when, Mr Messner?'

'We've got three shifts in the building,' Cyclops explained. 'The morning shift is eight a.m. to four p.m.
The afternoon shift is four p.m. to midnight. And the
graveyard shift is midnight to eight a.m.'

'Which shift is yours?' Kling asked.

'The graveyard shift. You just caught me, in fact. I'll be relieved here in ten minutes.'

'If you start work at midnight, what were you doing here at nine p.m. Monday?'

'Fellow who has the shift before mine went home sick. The super called me about eight o'clock, asked if I could come in early. I did him the favor. That was a long night, believe me.'

'It was an even longer night for Tinka Sachs,' Kling said.

'Yeah. Well, anyway, I took that fellow up at nine, nine-thirty, and he still hadn't come down by the time I was relieved.'

'At eight in the morning,' Carella said.

'That's right.'

'Is that usual?' Kling asked.

'What do you mean?'

'Did Tinka Sachs usually have men coming here who went up to her apartment at nine, nine-thirty and weren't down by eight the next morning?'

Cyclops blinked with his single eye. 'I don't like to talk about the dead,' he said.

'We're here precisely so you *can* talk about the dead,' Kling answered. 'And about the living who visited the dead. I asked a simple question, and I'd appreciate a simple answer. Was Tinka Sachs in the habit of entertaining men all night long?'

Cyclops blinked again. 'Take it easy, young fellow,' he said. 'You'll scare me right back into my elevator.'

Carella chose to laugh at this point, breaking the tension. Cyclops smiled in appreciation.

'You understand, don't you?' he said to Carella. 'What Mrs Sachs did up there in her apartment was *her* business, not anyone else's.'

'Of course,' Carella said. 'I guess my partner was just wondering why you weren't suspicious. About taking a man up who didn't come down again. That's all.'

'Oh,' Cyclops thought for a moment. Then he said, 'Well, I didn't give it a second thought.'

'Then it *was* usual, is that right?' Kling asked.

'I'm not saying it was usual, and I'm not saying it

wasn't. I'm saying if a woman over twenty-one wants to have a man in her apartment, it's not for me to say how long he should stay, all day or all night, it doesn't matter to me, sonny. You got that?'

'I've got it,' Kling said flatly.

'And I don't give a damn what they do up there, either, all day or all night, that's their business if they're old enough to vote. You got that, too?'

'I've got it,' Kling said.

'Fine,' Cyclops answered, and he nodded.

'Actually,' Carella said, 'the man didn't *have* to take the elevator down, did he? He could have gone up to the roof, and crossed over to the next building.'

'Sure,' Cyclops said. 'I'm only saying that neither me nor anybody else working in this building has the right to wonder about what anybody's doing up there or how long they're taking to do it, or whether they choose to leave the building by the front door or the roof or the steps leading to the basement or even by jumping out the window, it's none of our business. You close that door, you're private. That's my notion.'

'That's a good notion,' Carella said.

'Thank you.'

'You're welcome.'

'What'd the man look like?' Kling asked. 'Do you remember?'

'Yes, I remember,' Cyclops said. He glanced at Kling coldly, and then turned to Carella. 'Have you got a pencil and some paper?'

'Yes,' Carella said. He took a notebook and a slender gold pen from his inside jacket pocket. 'Go ahead.'

'He was a tall man, maybe six-two or six-three. He was blond. His hair was very straight, the kind of hair Sonny Tufts has, do you know him?'

'Sonny *Tufts?*' Carella said.

'That's right, the movie star, him. This fellow didn't look at all like him, but his hair was the same sort of straight blond hair.'

'What color were his eyes?' Kling asked.

'Didn't see them. He was wearing sunglasses.'

'At night?'

'Lots of people wear sunglasses at night nowadays,' Cyclops said.

'That's true,' Carella said.

'Like masks,' Cyclops added.

'Yes.'

'He was wearing sunglasses, and also he had a very deep tan, as if he'd just come back from down south someplace. He had on a light grey raincoat; it was drizzling a little Friday night, do you recall?'

'Yes, that's right,' Carella said. 'Was he carrying an umbrella?'

'No umbrella.'

'Did you notice any of his clothing under the raincoat?'

'His suit was a dark grey, charcoal grey, I could tell that by his trousers. He was wearing a white shirt—it showed up here, in the opening of the coat—and a black tie.'

'What color were his shoes?'

'Black.'

'Did you notice any scars or other marks on his face or hands?'

'No.'

'Was he wearing any rings?'

'A gold ring with a green stone on the pinky of his right hand—no, wait a minute, it was his left hand.'

'Any other jewelry you might have noticed? Cuff links, tie clasp?'

'No, I didn't see any.'

'Was he wearing a hat?'

'No hat.'

'Was he clean-shaven?'

'What do you mean?'

'Did he have a beard or a mustache?' Kling said.

'No. He was clean-shaven.'

'How old would you say he was?'

'Late thirties, early forties.'

'What about his build? Heavy, medium, or slight?'

'He was a big man. He wasn't fat, but he was a big man, muscular. I guess I'd have to say he was heavy. He had very big hands. I noticed the ring on his pinky looked very small for his hand. He was heavy, I'd say, yes, very definitely.'

'Was he carrying anything? Briefcase, suitcase, attaché—'

'Nothing.'

'Did he speak to you?'

'He just gave me the floor number, that's all. Nine, he said. That was all.'

'What sort of voice did he have? Deep, medium, high?'

'Deep.'

'Did you notice any accent or regional dialect?'

'He only said one word. He sounded like anybody else in the city.'

'I'm going to say that word several ways,' Carella said. 'Would you tell me which way sounded most like him?'

'Sure, go ahead.'

'Ny-un,' Carella said.

'Nope.'

'Noin.'

'Nope.'

'Nahn.'

'Nope.'

'Nan.'

'Nope.'

'Nine.'

'That's it. Straight out. No decorations.'

'Okay, good,' Carella said. 'You got anything else, Bert?'

'Nothing else,' Kling said.

'You're a very observant man,' Carella said to Cyclops.

'All I do every day is look at the people I take up and down,' Cyclops answered. He shrugged. 'It makes the job a little more interesting.'

'We appreciate everything you've told us,' Carella said. 'Thank you.'

'Don't mention it.'

Outside the building, Kling said, 'The snotty old bastard.'

'He gave us a lot,' Carella said mildly.

'Yeah.'

'We've really got a good description now.'

'*Too* good, if you ask me.'

'What do you mean?'

'The guy has one eye in his head, and one foot in the grave. So he reels off details even a trained observer would have missed. He might have been making up the whole thing, just to prove he's not a worthless old man.'

'Nobody's worthless,' Carella said mildly. 'Old or otherwise.'

'The humanitarian school of criminal detection,' Kling said.

'What's wrong with humanity?'

'Nothing. It was a human being who slashed Tinka Sachs to ribbons, wasn't it?' Kling asked.

And to this, Carella had no answer.

A good modeling agency serves as a great deal more than a booking office for the girls it represents. It provides an answering service for the busy young girl about town, a baby-sitting service for the working mother, a guidance-and-counseling service for the man-beleaguered model, a *pied-à-terre* for the harried and hurried between-sittings beauty.

Art and Leslie Cutler ran a good modeling agency. They ran it with the precision of a computer and the understanding of an analyst. Their offices were smart and walnut-paneled, a suite of three rooms on Carrington Avenue, near the bridge leading to Calm's Point. The address of the agency was announced over a doorway leading to a flight of carpeted steps. The address plate resembled a Parisian street sign, white enameled on a blue field, 21 Carrington, with the blue-carpeted steps beyond leading to the second story of the building. At the top of the stairs there was a second blue-and-white enameled sign, Paris again, except that this one was lettered in lowercase and it read, the cutlers.

Carella and Kling climbed the steps to the second floor, observed the chic nameplate without any noticeable show of appreciation, and walked into a small carpeted entrance foyer in which stood a white desk starkly fashionable against the walnut walls, nothing else. A girl sat behind the desk. She was astonishingly beautiful, exactly the sort of receptionist one would expect in a modeling agency; if she was only the receptionist, my God, what did the *models* look like?

'Yes, gentlemen, may I help you?' she asked. Her voice was Vassar out of finishing school out of country day. She wore eyeglasses with exaggerated black frames that did nothing whatever to hide the dazzling brilliance of her big blue eyes. Her makeup was subdued and wickedly innocent, a touch of pale pink on her lips, a blush of rose at her cheeks, the frames of her spectacles serving as liner for her eyes. Her hair was black and her smile was sunshine. Carella answered with a sunshine smile of his own, the one he usually reserved for movie queens he met at the governor's mansion.

'We're from the police,' he said. 'I'm Detective Carella; this is my partner, Detective Kling.'

'Yes?' the girl said. She seemed completely surprised to have policemen in her reception room.

'We'd like to talk to either Mr or Mrs Cutler,' Kling said. 'Are they in?'

'Yes, but what is this in reference to?' the girl asked.

'It's in reference to the murder of Tinka Sachs,' Kling said.

'Oh,' the girl said. 'Oh, yes.' She reached for a button on the executive phone panel, hesitated, shrugged, looked up at them with radiant blue-eyed innocence, and said, 'I suppose you have identification and all that.'

Carella showed her his shield. The girl looked expectantly at Kling. Kling sighed, reached into his pocket, and opened his wallet to where his shield was pinned to the leather.

'We never get detectives up here,' the girl said in explanation, and pressed the button on the panel.

'Yes?' a voice said.

'Mr Cutler, there are two detectives to see you, a Mr King and a Mr Coppola.'

'Kling and Carella,' Carella corrected.

'Kling and Capella,' the girl said.

Carella let it go.

'Ask them to come right in,' Cutler said.

'Yes, sir.' The girl clicked off and looked up at the

detectives. 'Won't you go in, please? Through the bull
pen and straight back.'

'Through the what?'

'The bull pen. Oh, that's the main office, you'll see it.
It's right inside the door there.' The telephone rang. The
girl gestured vaguely toward what looked like a solid
walnut wall, and then picked up the receiver. 'The
Cutlers,' she said. 'One moment, please.' She pressed a
button and then said, 'Mrs Cutler, it's Alex Jamison on
five-seven, do you want to take it?' She nodded, listened
for a moment, and then replaced the receiver. Carella and
Kling had just located the walnut knob on the walnut
door hidden in the walnut wall. Carella smiled sheepishly
at the girl (blue eyes blinked back radiantly) and opened
the door.

The bull pen, as the girl had promised, was just behind the reception room. It was a large open area with
the same basic walnut-and-white decor, broken by the
color of the drapes and the upholstery fabric on two
huge couches against the left-hand window wall. The
windows were draped in diaphanous saffron nylon, and
the couches were done in a complementary brown, the
fabric nubby and coarse in contrast to the nylon. Three
girls sat on the couches, their long legs crossed. All of
them were reading *Vogue*. One of them had her head inside a portable hair dryer. None of them looked up as
the men came into the room. On the right-hand side of
the room, a fourth woman sat behind a long white For-
mica counter, a phone to her ear, busily scribbling on a
pad as she listened. The woman was in her early forties,
with the unmistakable bones of an exmodel. She glanced
up briefly as Carella and Kling hesitated inside the doorway, and then went back to her jottings, ignoring them.

There were three huge charts affixed to the wall behind her. Each chart was divided into two-by-two-inch
squares, somewhat like a colorless checkerboard. Running down the extreme left-hand side of each chart was
a column of small photographs. Running across the top
of each chart was a listing for every working hour of the
day. The charts were covered with plexiglass panels, and
a black crayon pencil hung on a cord to the right of
each one. Alongside the photographs, crayoned onto

the charts in the appropriate time slots, was a record
and a reminder of any model's sittings for the week,
readable at a glance. To the right of the charts, and accessible through an opening in the counter, there was a
cubbyhole arrangement of mailboxes, each separate slot
marked with similar small photographs.

The wall bearing the door through which Carella and
Kling had entered was covered with eight-by-ten black-
and-white photos of every model the agency represent-
ed, some seventy-five in all. The photos bore no identifying names. A waist-high runner carried black crayon
pencils spaced at intervals along the length of the wall.
A wide white band under each photograph, plexiglass-
covered, served as the writing area for telephone messages. A model entering the room could, in turn, check
her eight-by-ten photo for any calls, her photo-marked
mailbox for any letters, and her photo-marked slot on
one of the three charts for her next assignment. Looking
into the room, you somehow got the vague impression
that photography played a major part in the business of
this agency. You also had the disquieting feeling that
you had seen all of these faces a hundred times before,
staring down at you from billboards and up at you from
magazine covers. Putting an identifying name under any
single one of them would have been akin to labeling the
Taj Mahal or the Empire State Building. The only naked wall was the one facing them as they entered, and it
—like the reception-room wall—seemed to be made of
solid walnut, with nary a door in sight.

'I think I see a knob,' Carella whispered, and they
started across the room toward the far wall. The woman
behind the counter glanced up as they passed, and then
pulled the phone abruptly from her ear with a 'Just a
second, Alex,' and said to the two detectives, 'Yes, may I
help you?'

'We're looking for Mr Cutler's office,' Carella said.

'Yes?' she said.

'Yes, we're detectives. We're investigating the murder
of Tinka Sachs.'

'Oh. Straight ahead,' the woman said. 'I'm Leslie Cutler.
I'll join you as soon as I'm off the phone.'

'Thank you,' Carella said. He walked to the walnut

wall, Kling following close behind him, and knocked on what he supposed was the door.

'Come in,' a man's voice said.

Art Cutler was a man in his forties with straight blond hair like Sunny Tufts, and with at least six feet four inches of muscle and bone that stood revealed in a dark blue suit as he rose beind his desk, smiling, and extended his hand.

'Come in, gentlemen,' he said. His voice was deep. He kept his hand extended while Carella and Kling crossed to the desk, and then he shook hands with each in turn, his grip firm and strong. 'Sit down, won't you?' he said, and indicated a pair of Saarinen chairs, one at each corner of his desk. 'You're here about Tinka,' he said dolefully.

'Yes,' Carella said.

'Terrible thing. A maniac must have done it, don't you think?'

'I don't know,' Carella said.

'Well, it *must* have been, don't you think?' he said to Kling.

'I don't know,' Kling said.

'That's why we're here, Mr Cutler,' Carella explained. 'To find out what we can about the girl. We're assuming that an agent would know a great deal about the people he repre—'

'Yes, that's true,' Cutler interrupted, 'and especially in Tinka's case.'

'Why especially in her case?'

'Well, we'd handled her career almost from the very beginning.'

'How long would that be, Mr Cutler?'

'Oh, at least ten years. She was only nineteen when we took her on, and she was . . . well, let me see, she was thirty in February, no, it'd be almost *eleven* years, that's right.'

'February what?' Kling asked.

'February third,' Cutler replied. 'She'd done a little modeling on the coast before she signed with us, but nothing very impressive. We got her into all the important magazines, *Vogue, Harper's, Mademoiselle*, well, you name them. Do you know what Tinka Sachs was earning?'

'No, what?' Kling said.

'Sixty dollars an hour. Multiply that by an eight- or ten-hour day, an average of six days a week, and you've got somewhere in the vicinity of a hundred and fifty thousand dollars a year.' Cutler paused. 'That's a lot of money. That's more than the president of the United States earns.'

'With none of the headaches,' Kling said.

'Mr Cutler,' Carella said, 'when did you last see Tinka Sachs alive?'

'Late Friday afternoon,' Cutler said.

'Can you give us the circumstances?'

'Well, she had a sitting at five, and she stopped in around seven to pick up her mail and to see if there had been any calls. That's all.'

'Had there?' Kling asked.

'Had there what?'

'Been any calls?'

'I'm sure I don't remember. The receptionist usually posts all calls shortly after they're received. You may have seen our photo wall—'

'Yes,' Kling said.

'Well, our receptionist takes care of that. If you want me to check with her, she may have a record, though I doubt it. Once a call is crayoned onto the wall—'

'What about mail?'

'I don't know if she had any or . . . wait a minute, yes, I think she did pick some up. I remember she was leafing through some envelopes when I came out of my office to chat with her.'

'What time did she leave here?' Carella asked.

'About seven-fifteen.'

'For another sitting?'

'No, she was heading home. She has a daughter, you know. A five-year-old.'

'Yes, I know,' Carella said.

'Well, she was going home,' Cutler said.

'Do you know where she lives?' Kling asked.

'Yes.'

'Where?'

'Stafford Place.'

'Have you ever been there?'

'Yes, of course.'

'How long do you suppose it would take to get from this office to her apartment?'

'No more than fifteen minutes.'

'Then Tinka would have been home by seven-thirty . . . *if* she went directly home.'

'Yes, I suppose so.'

'Did she say she was going directly home?'

'Yes. No, she said she wanted to pick up some cake, and *then* she was going home.'

'Cake?'

'Yes. There's a shop up the street that's exceptionally good. Many of our mannequins buy cakes and pastry there.'

'Did she say she was expecting someone later on in the evening?' Kling asked.

'No, she didn't say what her plans were.'

'Would your receptionist know if any of those telephone messages related to her plans for the evening?'

'I don't know, we can ask her.'

'Yes, we'd like to,' Carella said.

'What were *your* plans for last Friday night, Mr Cutler?' Kling asked.

'*My* plans?'

'Yes.'

'What do you mean?'

'What time did *you* leave the office?'

'Why would you possibly want to know *that?*' Cutler asked.

'You were the last person to see her alive,' Kling said.

'No, her *murderer* was the last person to see her alive,' Cutler corrected. 'And if I can believe what I read in the newspapers, her *daughter* was the *next*-to-last person to see her alive. So I really can't understand how Tinka's visit to the agency or *my* plans for the evening are in any way germane, or even related, to her death.'

'Perhaps they're not, Mr Cutler,' Carella said, 'but I'm sure you realize we're obliged to investigate every possibility.'

Cutler frowned, including Carella in whatever hostility he had originally reserved for Kling. He hesitated a moment and then grudgingly said, 'My wife and I joined some friends for dinner at *Les Trois Chats.*' He paused and added caustically, 'That's a French restaurant.'

'What time was that?' Kling asked.

'Eight o'clock.'

'Where were you at nine?'

'Still having dinner.'

'And at nine-thirty?'

Cutler sighed and said, 'We didn't leave the restaurant until a little after ten.'

'And then what did you do?'

'Really, is this necessary?' Cutler said, and scowled at the detectives. Neither of them answered. He sighed again and said, 'We walked along Hall Avenue for a while, and then my wife and I left our friends and took a cab home.'

The door opened.

Leslie Cutler breezed into the office, saw the expression on her husband's face, weighed the silence that greeted her entrance, and immediately said, 'What is it?'

'Tell them where we went when we left here Friday night,' Cutler said. 'The gentlemen are intent on playing cops and robbers.'

'You're joking,' Leslie said, and realized at once that they were not. 'We went to dinner with some friends,' she said quickly. 'Marge and Daniel Ronet—she's one of our mannequins. Why?'

'What time did you leave the restaurant, Mrs Cutler?'

'At ten.'

'Was your husband with you all that time?'

'Yes, of course he was.' She turned to Cutler and said, 'Are they allowed to do this? Shouldn't we call Eddie?'

'Who's Eddie?' Kling said.

'Our lawyer.'

'You won't need a lawyer.'

'Are you a new detective?' Cutler asked Kling suddenly.

'What's that supposed to mean?'

'It's supposed to mean your interviewing technique leaves something to be desired.'

'Oh? In what respect? What do you find lacking in my approach, Mr Cutler?'

'Subtlety, to coin a word.'

'That's very funny,' Kling said.

'I'm glad it amuses you.'

'Would it amuse you to know that the elevator operator at 791 Stafford Place gave us an excellent description of the man he took up to Tinka's apartment on the night she was killed? And would it amuse you further to know that the description fits you to a tee? How does *that* hit your funny bone, Mr Cutler?'

'I was nowhere near Tinka's apartment last Friday night.'

'Apparently not. I know you won't mind our contacting the friends you had dinner with, though—just to check.'

'The receptionist will give you their number,' Cutler said coldly.

'Thank you.'

Cutler looked at his watch. 'I have a lunch date,' he said. 'If you gentlemen are finished with your—'

'I wanted to ask your receptionist about those telephone messages,' Carella said. 'And I'd also appreciate any information you can give me about Tinka's friends and acquaintances.'

'My wife will have to help you with that.' Cutler glanced sourly at Kling and said, 'I'm not planning to leave town. Isn't that what you always warn a suspect not to do?'

'Yes, don't leave town,' Kling said.

'Bert,' Carella said casually, 'I think you'd better get back to the squad. Grossman promised to call with a lab report sometime this afternoon. One of us ought to be there to take it.'

'Sure,' Kling said. He went to the door and opened it. 'My partner's a little more subtle than I am,' he said, and left.

Carella, with his work cut out for him, gave a brief sigh, and said, 'Could we talk to your receptionist now, Mrs Cutler?'

Chapter Three

When Carella left the agency at two o'clock that Monday afternoon, he was in possession of little more than he'd had when he first climbed those blue-carpeted steps. The receptionist, radiating wide-eyed helpfulness, could not remember any of the phone messages that had been left for Tinka Sachs on the day of her death. She knew they were all personal calls, and she remembered that some of them were from men, but she could not recall any of the men's names. Neither could she remember the names of the women callers—yes, some of them were women, she said, but she didn't know exactly how many—nor could she remember why *any* of the callers were trying to contact Tinka.

Carella thanked her for her help, and then sat down with Leslie Cutler—who was still fuming over Kling's treatment of her husband—and tried to compile a list of men Tinka knew. He drew another blank here because Leslie informed him at once that Tinka, unlike most of the agency's mannequins (the word 'mannequin' was beginning to rankle a little) kept her private affairs to herself, never allowing a date to pick her up at the agency, and never discussing the men in her life, not even with any of the other mannequins (in fact, the word was beginning to rankle a lot). Carella thought at first that Leslie was suppressing information because of the jackass manner in which Kling had conducted the earlier interview. But as he questioned her more completely, he came to believe that she really knew nothing at all about Tinka's personal matters. Even on the few occasions when she and her husband had been invited to Tinka's home, it had been for a simple dinner for three, with no one else in attendance, and with the child Anna asleep in her own room. Comparatively charmed to pieces by Carella's patience after Kling's earlier display, Leslie offered him the agency flyer on Tinka, the composite that went to all photographers, advertising agency art directors, and prospective clients. He took it, thanked her, and left.

Sitting over a cup of coffee and a hamburger now, in a luncheonette two blocks from the squadroom, Carella took the composite out of its manila envelope and remembered again the way Tinka Sachs had looked the last time he'd seen her. The composite was an eight-by-ten black-and-white presentation consisting of a larger sheet folded in half to form two pages, each printed front and back with photographs of Tinka in various poses.

Carella studied the composite from first page to last.

The only thing the composite told him was that Tinka posed fully clothed, modeling neither lingerie nor swimwear, a fact he considered interesting, but hardly pertinent. He put the composite into the manila envelope, finished his coffee, and went back to the squadroom.

Kling was waiting and angry.

'What was the idea, Steve?' he asked immediately.

'Here's a composite on Tinka Sachs,' Carella said. 'We might as well add it to our file.'

'Never mind the composite. How about answering my question?'

'I'd rather not. Did Grossman call?'

'Yes. The only prints they've found in the room so far are the dead girl's. They haven't yet examined the knife, or her pocketbook. Don't try to get me off this, Steve. I'm goddamn good and sore.'

'Bert, I don't want to get into an argument with you. Let's drop it, okay?'

'No.'

'We're going to be working on this case together for what may turn out to be a long time. I don't want to start by—'

'Yes, that's right, and I don't like being ordered back to the squadroom just because someone doesn't like my line of questioning.'

'Nobody ordered you back to the squadroom.'

'Steve, you outrank me, and you told me to come back, and that was *ordering* me back. I want to know why.'

'Because you were behaving like a jerk, okay?'

'I don't think so.'

'Then maybe you ought to step back and take an objective look at yourself.'

'Damnit, it was *you* who said the old man's identification seemed reliable! Okay, so we walk into that office and we're face to face with the man who'd just been *described* to us! What'd you expect me to do? Serve him a cup of tea?'

'No, I expected you to accuse him—'

'Nobody accused him of anything!'

'—of murder and take him right up here to book him,' Carella said sarcastically. '*That's* what I expected.'

'I asked perfectly reasonable questions!'

You asked questions that were snotty and surly and hostile and amateurish. You treated him like a criminal from go, when you had no reason to. You immediately put him on the defensive instead of disarming him. If I were in his place, I'd have lied to you just out of spite. You made an enemy instead of a friend out of someone who might have been able to help us. That means if I need any further information about Tinka's professional life, I'll have to beg it from a man who now has good reason to hate the police.'

'He fit our description! Anyone would have asked—'

'Why the hell couldn't you ask in a civil manner? And *then* check on those friends he said he was with, and *then* get tough if you had something to work with? What did you accomplish your way? Not a goddamn thing. Okay, you asked me, so I'm telling you. I had work to do up there, and I couldn't afford to waste more time while you threw mud at the walls. *That's* why I sent you back here. Okay? Good. Did you check Cutler's alibi?'

'Yes.'

'*Was* he with those people?'

'Yes.'

'And *did* they leave the restaurant at ten and walk around for a while?'

'Yes.'

'Then Cutler couldn't have been the man Cyclops took up in his elevator.'

'Unless Cyclops got the time wrong.'

'That's a possibility, and I suggest we check it. But

the checking should have been done *before* you started hurling accusations around.'

'I didn't accuse anybody of anything!'

'Your entire approach did! Who the hell do you think you are, a Gestapo agent? You can't go marching into a man's office with nothing but an idea and start—'

'I was doing my best!' Kling said. 'If that's not good enough, you can go to hell.'

'It's not good enough,' Carella said, 'and I don't plan to go to hell, either.'

'I'm asking Pete to take me off this,' Kling said.

'He won't.'

'Why not?'

'Because I outrank you, like you said, and *I* want you on it.'

'Then don't ever try that again, I'm warning you. You embarrass me in front of a civilian again and—'

'If you had any sense, you'd have been embarrassed long before I asked you to go.'

'Listen, Carella—'

'Oh, it's *Carella* now, huh?'

'I don't have to take any crap from you, just remember that. I don't care what your badge says. Just remember I don't have to take any crap from you.'

'Or from anybody.'

'Or from anybody, right.'

'I'll remember.'

'See that you do,' Kling said, and he walked through the gate in the slatted railing and out of the squadroom.

Carella clenched his fists, unclenched them again, and then slapped one open hand against the top of his desk.

Detective Meyer Meyer came out of the men's room in the corridor, zipping up his fly. He glanced to his left toward the iron-runged steps and cocked his head, listening to the angry clatter of Kling's descending footfalls. When he came into the squadroom, Carella was leaning over, straight-armed, on his desk. A dead, cold expression was on his face.

'What was all the noise about?' Meyer asked.

'Nothing,' Carella said. He was seething with anger, and the word came out as thin as a razor blade.

'Kling again?' Meyer asked.

'Kling again.'

'Boy,' Meyer said, and shook his head, and said nothing more.

On his way home late that afternoon. Carella stopped at the Sachs apartment, showed his shield to the patrolman still stationed outside her door, and then went into the apartment to search for anything that might give him a line on the men Tinka Sachs had known—correspondence, a memo pad, an address book, anything. The apartment was empty and still. The child Anna Sachs had been taken to the Children's Shelter on Saturday and then released into the custody of Harvey Sadler— who was Tinka's lawyer—to await the arrival of the little girl's father from Arizona. Carella walked through the corridor past Anna's room, the same route the murderer must have taken, glanced in through the open door at the rows of dolls lined up in the bookcase, and then went past the room and into Tinka's spacious bedroom. The bed had been stripped, the blood-stained sheets and blanket sent to the police laboratory. There had been blood stains on the drapes as well, and these too had been taken down and shipped off to Grossman. The windows were bare now, overlooking the rooftops below, the boats moving slowly on the River Dix. Dusk was coming fast, a reminder that it was still only April. Carella flicked on the lights and walked around the chalked outline of Tinka's body on the thick green carpet, the blood soaked into it and dried to an ugly brown. He went to an oval table serving as a desk on the wall opposite the bed, sat in the pedestal chair before it, and began rummaging through the papers scattered over its top. The disorder told him that detectives from Homicide had already been through all this and had found nothing they felt worthy of calling to his attention. He sighed and picked up an evelope with an airmail border, turned it over to look at the flap, and saw that it had come from Dennis Sachs—Tinka's ex-husband—in Rainfield, Arizona. Carella took the letter from the envelope, unfolded it, and began reading:

Tuesday, April 6

My darling Tinka—

Here I am in the middle of the desert, writing by the light of a flickering kerosene lamp, and listening to the howl of the wind outside my tent. The others are all asleep already. I have never felt farther away from the city—or from you.

I become more impatient with Oliver's project every day of the week, but perhaps that's because I know what you are trying to do, and everything seems insignificant beside your monumental struggle. Who cares whether or not the Hohokam traversed this desert on their way from Old Mexico? Who cares whether we uncover any of their lodges here? All I know is that I miss you enormously, and respect you, and pray for you. My only hope is that your ordeal will soon be ended, and we can go back to the way it was in the beginning, before the nightmare began, before our love was shattered.

I will call East again on Saturday. All my love to Anna...

...and to you.

Dennis

Carella refolded the letter and put it back into the envelope. He had just learned that Dennis Sachs was out in the desert on some sort of project involving the Hohokam, whoever the hell they were, and that apparently he was still carrying the torch for his ex-wife. But beyond that Carella also learned that Tinka had been going through what Dennis called a 'monumental struggle' and 'ordeal'. What ordeal? Carella wondered. What struggle? And what exactly was the 'nightmare' Dennis mentioned later in his letter? Or was the nightmare the struggle itself, the ordeal, and not something that predated it? Dennis Sachs had been phoned in Arizona this morning by the authorities at the Children's Shelter, and was presumably already on his way East. Whether he yet realized it or not, he would have a great many questions to answer when he arrived.

Carella put the letter in his jacket pocket and began leafing through the other correspondence on the desk. There were bills from the electric company, the telephone company, most of the city's department stores, the Diners' Club, and many of the local merchants. There was a letter from a woman who had done house cleaning for Tinka and who was writing to say she could no longer work for her because she and her family were moving back to Jamaica, B.W.I. There was a letter from the editor of one of the fashion magazines, outlining her plans for shooting the new Paris line with Tinka and several other mannequins that summer, and asking whether she would be avaliable or not. Carella read these cursorily, putting them into a small neat pile at one edge of the oval table, and then found Tinka's address book.

There were a great many names, addresses, and telephone numbers in the small red leather book. Some of the people listed were men. Carella studied each name carefully, going through the book several times. Most of the names were run-of-the-mill Georges and Franks and Charlies, while others were a bit more rare like Clyde and Adrian, and still others were pretty exotic like Rion and Dink and Fritz. None of them rang a bell. Carella closed the book, put it into his jacket pocket and went through the remainder of the papers on the desk. The only other item of interest was a partially completed poem in Tinka's handwriting:

> When I think of what I am
> And of what I might have been,
> I tremble.
> I fear the night.
> Throughout the day,
> I push from dragons conjured in the dark
> Why will they not

He folded the poem carefully and put it into his jacket pocket together with the address book. Then he rose, walked to the door, took a last look into the room, and snapped out the light. He went down the corridor toward the front door. The last pale light of day glanced through Anna's windows into her room, glowing feebly on the faces of her dolls lined up in rows on the bookcase shelves. He went into the room and gently lifted one of the dolls from the top shelf, replaced it, and then recognized another doll as the one Anna had been holding in her lap on Saturday when he'd talked to her. He lifted the doll from the shelf.

The patrolman outside the apartment was startled to see a grown detective rushing by him with a doll under his arm. Carella got into the elevator, hurriedly found what he wanted in Tinka's address book, and debated whether he should call the squad to tell where he was headed, possibly get Kling to assist him with the arrest. He suddenly remembered that Kling had left the squadroom early. His anger boiled to the surface again. The *hell* with him, he thought, and came out into the street at a trot, running for his car. His thoughts came in a disorderly jumble, one following the next, the brutality of it, the goddamn stalking animal brutality of it, should I try making the collar alone, God that poor kid listening to her mother's murder, maybe I ought to go back to the office first, get Meyer to assist, but suppose my man is getting ready to cut out, why doesn't Kling shape up. Oh God, slashed again and again. He started the car. The child's doll was on the seat beside him. He looked again at the name and address in Tinka's book. Well? he thought. Which? Get help or go it alone?

He stepped on the accelerator.

There was an excitement pounding inside him now, coupled with the anger, a high anticipatory clamor that drowned out whatever note of caution whispered automatically in his mind. It did not usually happen this way, there were usually weeks or months of drudgery. The surprise of his windfall, the idea of a sudden culmination to a chase barely begun, unleashed a wild energy inside him, forced his foot onto the gas pedal more firmly. His hands were tight on the wheel. He drove with a recklessness that would have brought a summons to a civilian, weaving in and out of traffic, hitting the horn and the brake, his hands and his feet a part of the machine that hurtled steadily downtown toward the address listed in Tinka's book.

He parked the car, and came out onto the sidewalk, leaving the doll on the front seat. He studied the name plates in the entrance hallway—yes, this was it. He pushed a bell button at random, turned the knob on the locked inside door when the answering buzz sounded. Swiftly he began climbing the steps to the third floor. On the second-floor landing, he drew his service revolver, a .38 Smith & Wesson Police Model 10. The gun had a two-inch barrel that made it virtually impossible to snag on clothing when drawn. It weighed only two ounces and was six and seven-eighths of an inch long, with a blue finish and a checked walnut Magna stock with the familiar S&W monogram. It was capable of firing six shots without reloading.

He reached the third floor and started down the hallway. The mailbox had told him the apartment number was 34. He found it at the end of the hall, and put his ear to the door, listening. He could hear the muted voices of a man and a woman inside the apartment. Kick it in, he thought. You've got enough for an arrest. Kick in the door, and go in shooting if necessary—he's your man. He backed away from the door. He braced himself against the corridor wall opposite the door, lifted his right leg high, pulling back the knee, and then stepped forward and simultaneously unleashed a piston kick, aiming for the lock high on the door.

The wood splintered, the lock ripped from the jamb, the door shot inward. He followed the opening door into the room, the gun leveled in his right hand. He saw only a big beautiful dark-haired woman sitting on a couch facing the door, her legs crossed, a look of startled surprise on her face. But he had heard a man from outside. Where—?

He turned suddenly. He had abruptly realized that the apartment fanned out on both sides of the entrance door, and that the man could easily be to his right or his left, beyond his field of vision. He turned naturally to the right because he was right-handed, because the gun was in his right hand, and made the mistake that could have cost him his life.

The man was on his left.

Carella heard the sound of his approach too late, reversed his direction, caught a single glimpse of straight blond hair like Sonny Tufts, and then felt something hard and heavy smashing into his face.

Chapter Four

There was no furniture in the small room, save for a wooden chair to the right of the door. There were two windows on the wall facing the door, and these were covered with drawn green shades. The room was perhaps twelve feet wide by fifteen long, with a radiator in the center of one of the fifteen-foot walls.

Carella blinked his eyes and stared into the semidark-ness.

There were nighttime noises outside the windows, and he could see the intermittent flash of neon around the edges of the drawn shades. He wondered what time it was. He started to raise his left hand for a look at his watch, and discovered that it was handcuffed to the ra-diator. The handcuffs were his own. Whoever had closed the cuff onto his wrist had done so quickly and viciously; the metal was biting sharply into his flesh. The other cuff was clasped shut around the radiator leg. His watch was gone, and he seemed to have been stripped as well of his service revolver, his billet, his cartridges, his wallet and loose change, and even his shoes and socks. The side of his face hurt like hell. He lifted his right hand in exploration and found that his cheek and temple were crusted with dried blood. He looked down again at the radiator leg around which the second cuff was looped. Then he moved to the right of the radiator and looked behind it to see how it was fastened to the wall. If the fittings were loose—

He heard a key being inserted into the door lock. It suddenly occured to him that he was still alive, and the knowledge filled him with a sense of impending dread rather than elation. *Why* was he still alive? And was someone opening the door right this minute in order to remedy that oversight?

The key turned.

The overhead light snapped on.

A big brunette girl came into the room. She was the same girl who had been sitting on the couch when he'd bravely kicked in the front door. She was carrying a tray in her hands, and he caught the aroma of coffee the mo-ment she entered the room, that and the overriding scent of the heavy perfume the girl was wearing.

'Hello,' she said.

'Hello,' he answered.

'Have a nice sleep?'

'Lovely.'

She was very big, much bigger than she had seemed seated on the couch. She had the bones and body of a showgirl, five feet eight or nine inches tall, with firm full breasts threatening a low cut peasant blouse, solid thighs sheathed in a tight black skirt that ended just above her knees. Her legs were long and very white, shaped like a dancer's with full calves and slender ankles. She was wearing black slippers, and she closed the door behind her and came into the room silently, the slippers whispering across the floor.

She moved slowly, almost as though she were sleepwalking. There was a current of sensuality about her, emphasized by her dreamlike motion. She seemed to possess an acute awareness of her lush body, and this in turn seemed coupled with the knowledge that whatever she might be—housewife or whore, slattern or saint—men would try to do things to that body, and succeed, repeatedly and without mercy. She was a victim, and she moved with the cautious tread of someone who had been beaten before and now expects attack from any quarter. Her caution, her awareness, the ripeness of her body, the certain knowledge that it was available, the curious look of inevitability the girl wore, all invited further abuses, encouraged fantasies, drew dark imaginings from hidden corners of the mind. Rinsed raven-black hair framed the girl's white face. It was a face hard with knowledge. Smoky Cleopatra makeup shaded her eyes and lashes, hiding the deeper-toned flesh there. Her nose had been fixed once, a long time ago, but it was beginning to fall out of shape so that it looked now as if someone had broken it, and this too added to the victim's look she wore. Her mouth was brightly painted, a whore's mouth, a doll's mouth. It had said every word ever invented. It had done everything a mouth was ever forced to do.

'I brought you some coffee,' she said.

Her voice was almost a whisper. He watched her as she came closer. He had the feeling that she could kill a man as readily as kiss him, and he wondered again why he was still alive.

He noticed for the first time that there was a gun on the tray, alongside the coffee pot. The girl lifted the gun now, and pointed it at his belly, still holding the tray with one hand. 'Back,' she said.

'Why?'

'Don't fuck around with me,' she said. 'Do what I tell you to do when I tell you to do it.'

Carella moved back as far as his cuffed wrist would allow him. The girl crouched, the tight skirt riding up over her thighs, and pushed the tray toward the radiator. Her face was dead serious. The gun was a super .38-caliber Llama automatic. The girl held it steady in her right hand. The thumb safety on the left side of the gun had been thrown. The automatic was ready for firing.

The girl rose and backed away toward the chair near the entrance door, the gun still trained on him. She sat, lowered the gun, and said, 'go ahead.'

Carella poured coffee from the pot into the single mug on the tray. He took a swallow. The coffee was hot and strong.

'How is it?' the girl asked.

'Fine.'

'I made it myself.'

'Thank you.'

'I'll bring you a wet towel later,' she said. 'So you can wipe off that blood. It looks terrible.'

'It doesn't feel so hot, either,' Carella said.

'Well, who invited you?' the girl asked. She seemed about to smile, and then changed her mind.

'No one, that's true.' He took another sip of coffee. The girl watched him steadily.

'Steve Carella,' she said. 'Is that it?'

'That's right. What's *your* name?'

He asked the question quickly and naturally, but the girl did not step into the trap.

'Detective second/grade,' she said. '87th Squad.' She paused. 'Where's that?'

'Across from the park.'

'What park?'

'Grover Park.'

'Oh, yeah,' she said. 'That's a nice park. That's the nicest park in this whole damn city.'

'Yes,' Carella said.

'I saved your life, you know,' the girl said conversationally.

'Did you?'

'Yeah. *He* wanted to kill you.'

'I'm surprised he didn't.'

'Cheer up, maybe he will.'

'When?'

'You in a hurry?'

'Not particularly.'

The room went silent. Carella took another swallow of coffee. The girl kept staring at him. Outside, he could hear the sounds of traffic.

'What time is it?' he asked.

'About nine. Why? You got a date?'

'I'm wondering how long it'll be before I'm missed, that's all,' Carella said, and watched the girl.

'Don't try to scare me,' she said. 'Nothing scares me.'

'I wasn't trying to scare you.'

The girl scratched her leg idly, and then said, 'There's some questions I have to ask you.'

'I'm not sure I'll answer them.'

'You will,' she said. There was something cold and deadly in her voice. 'I can guarantee that. Sooner or later, you will.'

'Then it'll have to be later.'

'You're not being smart, mister.'

'I'm being very smart.'

'How?'

'I figure I'm alive only because you don't know the answers.'

'Maybe you're alive because I *want* you to be alive,' the girl said.

'Why?'

'I've never had anything like you before,' she said, and for the first time since she'd come into the room, she smiled. The smile was frightening. He could feel the flesh at the back of his neck beginning to crawl. He wet his lips and looked at her, and she returned his gaze steadily, the tiny evil smile lingering on her lips. 'I'm life or death to you,' she said. 'If I tell him to kill you, he will.'

'Not until you know all the answers,' Carella said.

'Oh, we'll get the answers. We'll have plenty of time to get the answers.' The smile dropped from her face. She put one hand inside her blouse and idly scratched her breast, and than looked at him again, and said, 'How'd you get here?'

'I took the subway.'

'That's a lie,' the girl said. There was no rancor in her voice. She accused him matter-of-factly, and then said, 'Your car was downstairs. The registration was in the glove compartment. There was also a sign on the sun visor, something about a law officer on a duty call.'

'All right, I drove here,' Carella said.

'Are you married?'

'Yes.'

'Do you have any children?'

'Two.'

'Girls?'

'A girl and a boy.'

'Then that's who the doll is for,' the girl said.

'What doll?'

'The one that was in the car. On the front seat of the car.'

'Yes,' Carella lied. 'It's for my daughter. Tomorrow's her birthday.'

'He brought it upstairs. It's outside in the living room.' The girl paused. 'Would you like to give your daughter that doll?'

'Yes.'

'Would you like to see her ever again?'

'Yes.'

'Then answer whatever I ask you, without any more lies about the subway or anything.'

'What's my guarantee?'

'Of what?'

'That I'll stay alive.'

'*I'm* your guarantee.'

'Why should I trust you?'

'You have to trust me,' the girl said. 'You're mine.' And again she smiled, and again he could feel the hairs stiffening at the back of his neck.

She got out of the chair. She scratched her belly, and then moved toward him, that same slow and cautious movement, as though she expected someone to strike her and was bracing herself for the blow.

'I haven't got much time,' she said. 'He'll be back soon.'

'Then what?'

The girl shrugged. 'Who knows you're here?' she asked suddenly.

Carella did not answer.

'How'd you get to us?'

Again, he did not answer.

'Did somebody see him leaving Tinka's apartment?'

Carella did not answer.

'How did you know where to come?'

Carella shook his head.

'Did someone identify him? How did you trace him?'

Carella kept watching her. She was standing three feet away from him now, too far to reach, the Llama dangling loosely in her right hand. She raised the gun.

'Do you want me to shoot you?' she asked conversationally.

'No.'

'I'll aim for your balls, would you like that?'

'No.'

'Then answer my questions.'

'You're not going to kill me,' Carella said. He did not take his eyes from the girl's face. The gun was pointed at his groin now, but he did not look at her finger curled inside the trigger guard.

The girl took a step closer. Carella crouched near the radiator, unable to get to his feet, his left hand manacled close to the floor. 'I'll enjoy this,' the girl promised, and struck him suddenly with the butt of the heavy gun, turning the butt up swiftly as her hand lashed out. He felt the numbing shock of metal against bone as the automatic caught him on the jaw and his head jerked back.

'You like?' the girl asked.

He said nothing.

'You *no* like, huh, baby?' She paused. 'How'd you find us?'

Again, he did not answer. She moved past him swiftly, so that he could not turn in time to stop the blow that came from behind him, could not kick out at her as he had planned to do the next time she approached. The butt caught him on the ear, and he felt the cartilage tearing as the metal rasped downward. He whirled toward her angrily, grasping at her with his right arm as he turned, but she danced out of his reach and around to the front of him again, and again hit him with the automatic, cutting him over the left eye this time. He felt the blood start down his face from the open gash.

'What do you say?' she asked.

'I say go to hell,' Carella said, and the girl swung the gun again. He thought he was ready for her this time. But she was only feinting, and he grabbed out at empty air as she moved swiftly to his right out of reach. The manacled hand threw him off balance. He fell forward, reaching for support with his free hand, the handcuff biting sharply into his other wrist. The gun butt caught him again just as his hand touched the floor. He felt it colliding with the base of his skull, a two-pound-six-and-a-half-ounce weapon swung with all the force of the girl's substantial body behind it. The pain shot clear to the top of his head. He blinked his eyes against the sudden dizziness. Hold on, he told himself, hold on, and was suddenly nauseous. The vomit came up into his throat, and he brought his right hand to his mouth just as the girl hit him again. He fell back dizzily against the radiator. He blinked up at the girl. Her lips were pulled back taut over her teeth, she was breathing harshly, the gun hand went back again, he was too weak to turn his head aside. He tried to raise his right arm, but it fell limply into his lap.

'Who saw him?' the girl asked.

'No,' he mumbled.

'I'm going to break your nose,' she said. Her voice sounded very far away. He tried to hold the floor for support, but he wasn't sure where the floor was any more. The room was spinning. He looked up at the girl and saw her spinning face and breasts, smelled the heavy cloying perfume and saw the gun in her hand. 'I'm going to break your nose, mister.'

'No.'

'Yes,' she said.

'No.'

He did not see the gun this time. He felt only the excruciating pain of bones splintering. His head rocked back with the blow, colliding with the cast-iron ribs of the radiator. The pain brought him back to raging consciousness. He lifted his right hand to his nose, and the girl hit him again, at the base of the skull again, and again he felt sensibility slipping away from him. He smiled stupidly. She would not let him die, and she would not let him live. She would not allow him to become unconscious, and she would not allow him to regain enough strength to defend himself.

'I'm going to knock out all of your teeth,' the girl said.

He shook his head.

'Who told you where to find us? Was it the elevator operator? Was it that one-eyed bastard?'

He did not answer.

'Do you want to lose all your teeth?'

'No.'

'Then tell me.'

'No.'

'You have to tell me,' she said. 'You *belong* to me.'

'No,' he said.

There was a silence. He knew the gun was coming again. He tried to raise his hand to his mouth, to protect his teeth, but there was no strength in his arm. He sat with his left wrist caught in the fierce biting grip of the handcuff, swollen, throbbing, with blood pouring down his face and from his nose, his nose a throbbing mass of splintered bone, and waited for the girl to knock out his teeth as she had promised, helpless to stop her.

He felt her lips upon him.

She kissed him fiercely and with her mouth open, her tongue searching his lips and his teeth. Then she pulled away from him, and he heard her whisper, 'In the morning, they'll find you dead.'

He lost consciousness again.

On Tuesday morning, they found the automobile at the bottom of a steep cliff some fifty miles across the River Harb, in a sparsely populated area of the adjoining state. Most of the paint had been burned away by what must have been an intensely hot fire, but it was still

possible to tell that the car was a green 1961 Pontiac se-
dan bearing the license plate RI 7-3461.

The body on the front seat of the car had been incinerated. They knew by what remained of the lower por-
tions that the body had once been a man, but the face
and torso had been cooked beyond recognition, the hair
and clothing gone, the skin black and charred, the arms
drawn up into the typical pugilistic attitude caused by
post-mortem contracture of burned muscles, the fingers
hooked like claws. A gold wedding band was on the
third finger of the skeletal left hand. The fire had eaten
away the skin and charred the remaining bones and
turned the gold of the ring to a dull black. A .38 Smith &
Wesson was caught in the exposed springs of the front seat,
together with the metal parts that remained of what once
had been a holster.

All of the man's teeth were missing from his mouth.

In the cinders of what they supposed had been his
wallet, they found a detective's shield with the identifying number 714-5632

A call to headquarters across the river informed the
investigating police that the shield belonged to a detective second/grade named Stephen Louis Carella.

Chapter Five

Teddy Carella sat in silence of her living room and
watched the lips of Detective Lieutenant Peter Byrnes as
he told her that her husband was dead. The scream
welled up into her throat, she could feel the muscles there
contracting until she thought she would strangle. She
brought her hand to her mouth, her eyes closed tight so
that she would no longer have to watch the words that
formed on the lieutenant's lips, no longer have to see the
words that confirmed what she had known was true
since the night before when her husband had failed to
come home for dinner.

She would not scream, but a thousand screams
echoed inside her head. She felt faint. She almost

swayed out of the chair, and then she looked up into the lieutenant's face as she felt his supporting arm around her shoulders. She nodded. She tried to smile up at him sympathetically, tried to let him know she realized this was an unpleasant task for him. But the tears were streaming down her face and she wished only that her husband were there to comfort her, and then abruptly she realized that her husband would never be there to comfort her again, the realization circling back upon itself, the silent screams ricocheting inside her.

The lieutenant was talking again.

She watched his lips. She sat stiff and silent in the chair, her hands clasped tightly in her lap, and wondered where the children were, how would she tell the children, and saw the lieutenant's lips as he said his men would do everything possible to uncover the facts of her husband's death. In the meantime, Teddy, if there's anything I can do, anything I can do personally, I mean, I think you know how much Steve meant to me, to all of us, if there's anything Harriet or I can do to help in any way, Teddy, I don't have to tell you we'll do anything we can, anything.

She nodded.

There's a possibility this was just an accident, Teddy, though we doubt it, we think he was, we don't think it was an accident, why would he be across the river in the next state, fifty miles from here?

She nodded again. Her vision was blurred by the tears. She could barely see his lips as he spoke.

Teddy, I loved that boy. I would rather have a bullet in my heart than be here in this room today with this, with this information. I'm sorry. Teddy I am sorry.

She sat in the chair as still as a stone.

Detective Meyer Meyer left the squadroom at two p.m. and walked across the street and past the low stone wall leading into the park. It was a fine April day, the sky a clear blue, the sun shining overhead, the birds chirping in the newly leaved trees.

He walked deep into the park, and found an empty bench and sat upon it, crossing his legs, one arm stretched out across the top of the bench, the other hanging loose in his lap. There were young boys and girls holding hands and whispering nonsense, there were children chasing each other and laughing, there were nannies wheeling baby carriages, there were old men reading books as they walked, there was the sound of a city hovering on the air.

There was life.

Meyer Meyer sat on the bench and quietly wept for his friend.

Detective Cotton Hawes went to a movie.

The movie was a western. There was a cattle drive in it, thousands of animals thundering across the screen, men sweating and shouting, horses rearing, bullwhips cracking. There was also an attack on a wagon train, Indians circling, arrows and spears whistling through the air, guns answering, men screaming. There was a fight in a saloon, too, chairs and bottles flying, tables collapsing, women running for cover with their skirts pulled high, fists connecting. Altogether, there was noise and color and loud music and plenty of action.

When the end titles flashed onto the screen, Hawes rose and walked up the aisle and out into the street.

Dusk was coming.

The city was hushed.

He had not been able to forget that Steve Carella was dead.

Andy Parker, who had hated Steve Carella's guts when he was alive, went to bed with a girl that night. The girl was a prostitute, and he got into her bed and her body by threatening to arrest her if she didn't come across. The girl had been hooking in the neighborhood for little more than a week. The other working hustlers had taken her aside and pointed out all the Vice Squad bulls and also all the local plainclothes fuzz so that she wouldn't make the mistake of propositioning one of them. But Parker had been on sick leave for two weeks with pharyngitis and had not been included in the girl's original briefing by her colleagues. She had approached what looked like a sloppy drunk in a bar on Ainsley, and before the bartender could catch her eye to warn her, she had given him the familiar 'Wanna have some fun, baby?' line and then had compounded the error by telling Parker it would cost him a fin for a single roll in the hay or twenty-five bucks for all night. Parker had accepted the girl's proposition, and had left the bar with her while the owner of the place frantically signaled his warning. The girl didn't know why the hell he was waving his arms at her. She knew only that she had a John who said he wanted to spend the night with her. She didn't know the John's last name was Law.

She took Parker to a rented room on Culver. Parker was very drunk—he had begun drinking at twelve noon when word of Carella's death reached the squadroom— but he was not drunk enough to forget that he could not arrest this girl until she exposed her 'privates'. He waited until she took off her clothes, and then he showed her his shield and said she could take her choice, a possible three years in the jug, or a pleasant hour or two with a very nice fellow. The girl, who had met very nice fellows like Parker before, all of whom had been Vice Squad cops looking for fleshy handouts, figured this was only a part of her normal overhead, nodded briefly, and spread out on the bed for him.

Parker was very very drunk.

To the girl's great surprise, he seemed more interested in talking than in making love, as the euphemism goes.

'What's the sense of it all, would you tell me?' he said, but he did not wait for an answer. 'Son of a bitch like Carella gets cooked in a car by some son of a bitch, what's the sense of it? You know what I see every day of the week, you know what we *all* of us see every day of the week, how do you expect us to stay human, would you tell me? Son of a bitch gets cooked like that, doing his job is all, how do you expect us to stay human? What am I doing here with you, a two-bit whore, is that something for me to be doing? I'm a nice fellow. Don't you know I'm a nice fellow?'

'Sure, you're a nice fellow,' the girl said, bored.

'Garbage every day,' Parker said. 'Filth and garbage, I have the stink in my nose when I go home at night. You know where I live? I live in a garden apartment in Majesta. I've got three and a half rooms, a nice little kitchen, you know, a nice apartment. I've got a hi-fi set and also I belong to the Classics Club. I've got all those books by the big writers, the important writers. I haven't got much time to read them, but I got them all there on a shelf, you should see the books I've got. There are nice people living in that apartment building, not like here, not like what you find in this crumby precinct, how old are you anyway, what are you nineteen, twenty?'

'I'm twenty-one,' the girl said.

'Sure, look at you, the shit of the city.'

'Listen, mister—'

'Shut up, shut up, who the hell's asking you? I'm *paid* to deal with it, all the shit that gets washed into the sewers, that's my job. My neighbors in the building know I'm a detective, they respect me, they look up to me. They don't know that all I do is handle shit all day long until I can't stand the stink of it any more. The kids riding their bikes in the courtyard, they all say, "Good morning, Detective Parker." That's me, a detective. They watch television, you see. I'm one of the good guys. I carry a gun. I'm brave. So look what happens to that son of a bitch Carella. What's the sense?'

'I don't know what you're talking about,' the girl said.

'What's the sense, what's the sense?' Parker said. 'People, boy, I could tell you about people. You wouldn't believe what I could tell you about people.'

'I've been around a little myself,' the girl said drily.

'You can't blame me,' he said suddenly.

'What?'

'You can't blame me. It's not my fault.'

'Sure. Look, mister, I'm a working girl. You want some of this, or not? Because if you—'

'Shut up, you goddamn whore, don't tell me what to do.'

'Nobody's—'

'I can pull you in and make your life miserable, you little slut. I've got the power of life and death over you, don't forget it.'

'Not quite,' the girl said with dignity.

'Not quite, not quite, don't give me any of that crap.'

'You're drunk,' the girl said. 'I don't even think you can—'

'Never mind what I am, I'm not drunk.' He shook his head. 'All right, I'm drunk, what the hell do you care what I am? You think I care what *you* are? You're *nothing* to me, you're *less* than nothing to me.'

'Then what are you doing here?'

'Shut up,' he said. He paused. 'The kids all yell good morning at me,' he said.

He was silent for a long time. His eyes were closed. The girl thought he had fallen asleep. She started to get off the bed, and he caught her arm and pulled her down roughly beside him.

'Stay where you are.'

'Okay,' she said. 'But look, you think we could get this over with? I mean it, mister, I've got a long night ahead of me. I got expenses to meet.'

'Filth,' Parker said. 'Filth and garbage.'

'Okay, already, filth and garbage, do you want it not?'

'He was a good cop,' Parker said suddenly.

'What?'

'He was a good cop,' he said again, and rolled over quickly and put his head into the pillow.

Chapter Six

At seven-thirty Wednesday morning, the day after the burned wreckage was found in the adjoining state, Bert Kling went back to the apartment building on Stafford Place, hoping to talk again to Ernest Cyclops Messner. The lobby was deserted when he entered the building.

If he had felt alone the day that Claire Townsend was murdered, if he had felt alone the day he held her in his arms in a bookshop demolished by gunfire, suddenly bereft in a world gone cold and senselessly cruel, he now felt something curiously similar and yet enormously different.

Steve Carella was dead.

The last words he had said to the man who had been his friend were angry words. He could not take them back now, he could not call upon a dead man, he could not offer apologies to a corpse. On Monday, he had left the squadroom earlier than he should have, in anger, and sometime that night Carella had met his death. And now there was a new grief within him, a new feeling of helplessness, but it was coupled with an overriding desire to set things right again—for Carella, for Claire, he did not really know. He knew he could not reasonably blame himself for what had happened, but neither could he stop blaming himself. He had to talk to Cyclops again. Perhaps there was something further the man could tell him. Perhaps Carella had contacted him again that Monday night, and uncovered new information that had sent him rushing out to investigate alone.

The elevator doors opened. The operator was not Cyclops.

'I'm looking for Mr Messner,' Kling told the man. 'I'm from the police.'

'He's not here,' the man said.

'He told us he has the graveyard shift.'

'Yeah, well, he's not here.'

'It's only seven-thirty,' Kling said.

'I know what time it is.'

'Well, where is he, can you tell me that?'

'He lives someplace here in the city,' the man said, 'but I don't know where.'

'Thank you,' Kling said, and left the building.

It was still too early in the morning for the rush of white-collar workers to subways and buses. The only people in the streets were factory workers hurrying to punch an eight-a.m. timeclock; the only vehicles were delivery trucks and an occasional passenger car. Kling walked swiftly, looking for a telephone booth. It was going to be another beautiful day; the city had been blessed with lovely weather for the past week now. He saw an open drugstore on the next corner, a telephone plaque fastened to the brick wall outside. He went into the store and headed for the directories at the rear.

Ernest Cyclops Messner lived at 1117 Gainesborough Avenue in Riverhead, not far from the County Court Building. The shadow of the elevated-train structure fell over the building, and the frequent rumble of trains pulling in and out of the station shattered the silence of the street. But it was a good low-to-middle-income residential area, and Messner's building was the newest on the block. Kling climbed the low flat entrance steps, went into the lobby, and found a listing for E. Messner. He rang the bell under the mailbox, but there was no answering buzz. He tried another bell. A buzz sounded, releasing the lock mechanism on the inner lobby door. He pushed open the door, and began climbing to the seventh floor. It was a little after eight a.m., and the building still seemed asleep.

He was somewhat winded by the time he reached the seventh floor. He paused on the landing for a moment, and then walked into the corridor, looking for apartment 7A. He found it just off the stairwell, and rang the bell.

There was no answer.

He rang the bell again.

He was about to ring it a third time when the door to the apartment alongside opened and a young girl rushed out, looking at her wrist watch and almost colliding with Kling.

'Oh, hi,' she said, surprised. 'Excuse me.'

'That's all right.' He reached for the bell again. The girl had gone past him and was starting down the steps. She turned suddenly.

'Are you looking for Mr Messner?' she asked.

'Yes, I am.'

'He isn't home.'

'How do you know?'

'Well, he doesn't get home until about nine,' she said. 'He works nights, you know.'

'Does he live here alone?'

'Yes, he does. His wife died a few years back. He's lived here a long time, I know him from when I was a little girl.' She looked at her watch again. 'Listen, I'm going to be late. Who *are* you, anyway?'

'I'm from the police,' Kling said.

'Oh, hi.' The girl smiled. 'I'm Marjorie Gorman.'

'Would you know where I can reach him, Marjorie?'

'Did you try his building? He works in a fancy apartment house on—'

'Yes, I just came from there.'

'Wasn't he there?'

'No.'

'That's funny,' Marjorie said. 'Although, come to think of it, we didn't hear him last night, either.'

'What do you mean?'

'The television. The walls are very thin, you know. When he's home, we can hear the television going.'

'Yes, but he works nights.'

'I mean before he leaves. He doesn't go to work until eleven o'clock. He starts at midnight, you know.'

'Yes, I know.'

'Well, that's what I meant. Listen, I really do have to hurry. If you want to talk, you'll have to walk me to the station.'

'Okay,' Kling said, and they started down the steps. 'Are you sure you didn't hear the television going last night?'

'I'm positive.'

'Does he usually have it on?'

'Oh, *con*stantly,' Marjorie said. 'He lives alone, you know, the poor old man. He's got to do *some*thing with his time.'

'Yes, I suppose so.'

'Why did you want to see him?'

She spoke with a pronounced Riverhead accent that somehow marred her clean good looks. She was a tall girl, perhaps nineteen years old, wearing a dark-grey suit and a white blouse, her auburn hair brushed back behind her ears, the lobes decorated with tiny pearl earrings.

'There are some things I want to ask him,' Kling said.

'About the Tinka Sachs murder?'

'Yes.'

'He was telling me about that just recently.'

'When was that?'

'Oh, I don't know. Let me think.' They walked out of

the lobby and into the street. Marjorie had long legs, and she walked very swiftly. Kling, in fact, was having trouble keeping up with her. 'What's today, anyway?'

'Wednesday,' Kling said.

'Wednesday, mmm, boy where does the week go? It must have been Monday. That's right. When I got home from the movies Monday night, he was downstairs putting out his garbage. So we talked awhile. He said he was expecting a detective.'

'A detective? Who?'

'What do you mean?'

'Did he say *which* detective he was expecting? Did he mention a name?'

'No, I don't think so. He said he'd talked to some detectives just that morning—that was Monday, right?—and that he'd got a call a few minutes ago saying another detective was coming up to see him.'

'Did he say that exactly? That *another* detective was coming up to see him? A *different* detective?'

'Oh. I don't know if he said just that. I mean, it could have been one of the detectives he'd talked to that morning. I really don't know for sure.'

'Does the name Carella mean anything to you?'

'No.' Marjorie paused. 'Should it?'

'Did Mr Messner use that name when he was talking about the detective who was coming to see him?'

'No, I don't think so. He only said he'd had a call from a detective, that was all. He seemed very proud. He told me they probably wanted him to describe the man again, the one he saw going up to her apartment. The dead girl's. Brrrr, it gives you the creeps, doesn't it?'

'Yes,' Kling said. 'It does.'

They were approaching the elevated station now. They paused at the bottom of the steps.

'This was Monday afternoon, you say?'

'No. Monday night. Monday *night*, I said.'

'What time Monday night?'

'About ten-thirty, I guess. I told you, I was coming home from the movies.'

'Let me get this straight,' Kling said. 'At ten-thirty Monday night, Mr Messner was putting out his garbage, and he told you he had just received a call from a detective who was on his way over? Is that it?'

'That's it.' Marjorie frowned. 'It *was* kind of late, wasn't it? I mean, to be making a business visit. Or do you people work that late?'

'Well, yes, but . . .' Kling shook his head.

'Listen, I really have to go,' Marjorie said. 'I'd like to talk to you, but—'

'I'd appreciate a few more minutes of your time, if you can—'

'Yes, but my boss—'

'I'll call him later and explain.'

'Yeah, you don't *know* him,' Marjorie said, and rolled her eyes.

'Can you just tell me whether Mr Messner mentioned anything about this detective the next time you saw him. I mean, *after* the detective was there.'

'Well, I haven't seen him since Monday night.'

'You didn't see him at *all* yesterday?'

'Nope. Well, I usually miss him in the morning, you know, because I'm gone before he gets home. But sometimes I drop in at night, just to say hello, or he'll come in for something, you know, like that. And I told you about the television. We just didn't hear it. My mother commented about it, as a matter of fact. She said Cyclops was probably—that's what we call him, Cyclops, everybody does, he doesn't mind—she said Cyclops was probably out on the town.'

'Does he often go out on the town?'

'Well, I don't think so—but who knows? Maybe he felt like having himself a good time, you know? Listen, I really have to—'

'All right, I won't keep you. Thank you very much, Marjorie. If you'll tell me where you work, I'll be happy to—'

'Oh, the hell with him. I'll tell him what happened, and he can take it or leave it. I'm thinking of quitting, anyway.'

'Well, thank you again.'

'Don't mention it,' Marjorie said, and went up the steps to the platform.

Kling thought for a moment, and then searched in his

pocket for a dime. He went into the cafeteria on the corner, found a phone booth, and identified himself to the operator, telling her he wanted the listing for the lobby phone in Tinka's building on Stafford Place. She gave him the number, and he dialed it. A man answered the phone. Kling said, 'I'd like to talk to the superintendent, please.'

'This is the super.'

'This is Detective Kling of the 87th Squad,' Kling said. 'I'm investigating—'

'Who?' the superintendent said.

'Detective Kling. Who's this I'm speaking to?'

'I'm the super of the building. Emmanuel Farber. Manny. Did you say this was a detective?'

'That's right.'

'Boy, when are you guys going to give us some rest here?'

'What do you mean?'

'Don't you have nothing to do but call up here?'

'I haven't called you before, Mr Farber.'

'No, not you, never mind. This phone's been going like sixty.'

'Who called you?'

'Detectives, never mind.'

'Who? Which detectives?'

'The other night.'

'When?'

'Monday. Monday night.'

'A detective called you Monday night?'

'Yeah, wanted to know where he could reach Cyclops. That's one of our elevator operators.'

'Did you tell him?'

'Sure, I did.'

'Who was he? Did he give you his name?'

'Yeah, some Italian fellow.'

Kling was silent for a moment.

'Would the name have been Carella?' he asked.

'That's right.'

'Carella?'

'Yep, that's the one.'

'What time did he call?'

'Oh, I don't know. Sometime in the evening.'

'And he said his name was Carella?'

'That's right, Detective Carella, that's what he said. Why? You know him?'

'Yes,' Kling said. I know him.'

'Well, you ask him. He'll tell you.'

'What time in the evening did he call? Was it early or late?'

'What do you mean by early or late?' Farber asked.

'Was it before dinner?'

'No. Oh no, it was after dinner. About ten o'clock, I suppose. Maybe a little later.'

'And what did he say to you?'

'He wanted Cyclops' address, said he had some questions to ask him.'

'About what?'

'About the murder.'

'He said that specifically? He said, "I have some questions to ask Cyclops about the murder"?'

'About the Tinka Sachs murder, is what he actually said.'

'He said, "This is Detective Carella, I want to know—" '

'That's right, this is Detective Carella—'

' "—I want to know Cyclops Messner's address because I have some questions to ask him about the Tinka Sachs murder." '

'No, that's not it exactly.'

'What's wrong with it?' Kling asked.

'He didn't say the name.'

'You just said he *did* say the name. The Tinka Sachs murder. You said—'

'Yes, that's right. That's not what I mean.'

'Look, what—?'

'He didn't say Cyclops' name.'

'I don't understand you.'

'All he said was he wanted the address of the one-eyed elevator operator because he had some questions to ask him about the Tinka Sachs murder. That's what he said.'

'He referred to him as the one-eyed elevator operator?'

'That's right.'

'You mean he didn't know the name?'

'Well, I don't know about that. He didn't know how to *spell* it, though, that's for sure.'

'Excuse me,' the telephone operator said. 'Five cents for the next five minutes, please.'

'Hold on,' Kling said. He reached into his pocket, and found only two quarters. He put one into the coin slot.

'Was that twenty-five cents you deposited, sir?' the operator asked.

'That's right.'

'If you'll let me have your name and address, sir, we'll—'

'No, forget it.'

'—send you a refund in stamps.'

'No, that's all right, operator, thank you. Just give me as much time as the quarter'll buy, okay?'

'Very well, sir.'

'Hello?' Kling said. 'Mr Farber?'

'I'm still here,' Farber said.

'What makes you think this detective couldn't spell Cyclops' name?'

'Well, I gave him the address, you see, and I was about to hang up when he asked me about the spelling. He wanted to know the correct spelling of the name.'

'And what did you say?'

'I said it was Messner, M-E-S-S-N-E-R, Ernest Messner, and I repeated the address for him again, 1117 Gainesborough Avenue in Riverhead.'

'And then what?'

'He said thank you very much and hung up.'

"Sir, was it your impression that he did not know Cyclops' name until you gave it to him?"

'Well, I couldn't say that for sure. All he wanted was the correct spelling.'

'Yes, but he asked for the address of the one-eyed elevator operator, isn't that what you said?'

'That's right.'

'If he knew the name, why didn't he use it?'

'You got me. What's *your* name?' the superintendent asked.

'Kling. Detective Bert Kling.'

'Mine's Farber, Emmanuel Farber, Manny.'

'Yes, I know. You told me.'

'Oh. Okay.'

There was a long silence on the line.

'Was that all, Detective Kling?' Farber said at last. 'I've got to get these lobby floors waxed and I'm—'

'Just a few more questions,' Kling said.

'Well, okay, but could we—?'

'Cyclops had his usual midnight-to-eight-a.m. shift Monday night, is that right?'

'That's right, but—'

'When he came to work, did he mention anything about having seen a detective?'

'He *didn't*,' Farber said.

'He didn't mention a detective at all? He didn't say—'

'No, he didn't come to work.'

'What?'

'He didn't come to work Monday nor yesterday, either,' Farber said. 'I had to get another man to take his place.'

'Did you try to reach him?'

'I waited until twelve-thirty, with the man he was supposed to relieve taking a fit, and finally I called his apartment, three times in fact, and there was no answer. So I phoned one of the other men. Had to run the elevator myself until the man got here. That must've been about two in the morning.'

'Did Cyclops contact you at all any time yesterday?'

'Nope. You think he'd call, wouldn't you?'

'Did he contact you today?'

'Nope.'

'But you're expecting him to report to work tonight, aren't you?'

'Well, he's due at midnight, but I don't know. I hope he shows up.'

'Yes, I hope so, too,' Kling said. 'Thank you very much, Mr Farber. You've been very helpful.'

'Sure thing,' Farber said, and hung up.

Kling sat in the phone booth for several moments, trying to piece together what he had just learned. Someone had called Farber on Monday night at about ten, identifying himself as Detective Carella, and asking for the address of the one-eyed elevator operator. Carella knew the man was named Ernest Messner and nicknamed Cyclops. He would not have referred to him as the one-eyed elevator operator. But more important than that, he would never have called the superintendent at all. Knowing the man's name, allegedly desiring his address, he would have done exactly what Kling had done this morning. He would have consulted the telephone directories and found a listing for Ernest Messner in the Riverhead book, as simple as that, as routine as that. No, the man who had called Farber was not Carella. But he had known Carella's name, and had made good use of it.

At ten-thirty Monday night, Marjorie Gorman had met Cyclops in front of the building and he had told her he was expecting a visit from a detective. That could only mean that 'Detective Carella' had already called Cyclops and told him he would stop by. And now, Cyclops was missing, had indeed been missing since Monday night.

Kling came out of the phone booth, and began walking back toward the building on Gainesborough Avenue.

The landlady of the building did not have a key to Mr Messner's apartment. Mr Messner has his own lock on the door, she said, the same as any of the other tenants in the building, and she certainly did not have a key to Mr Messner's lock, nor to the locks of any of the other tenants. Moreover, she would *not* grant Kling permission to try his skeleton key on the door, and she warned him that if he forced entry into Mr Messner's apartment, she would sue the city. Kling informed her that if she cooperated, she would save him the trouble of going all the way downtown for a search warrant, and she said she didn't *care* about his going all the way downtown, suppose Mr Messner came back and learned she had let the police in there while he was away, *who'd* get the lawsuit then, would he mind telling her?

Kling said he would go downtown for the warrant.

Go ahead then, the landlady told him.

It took an hour to get downtown, twenty minutes to obtain the warrant, and another hour to get back to Riverhead again. His skeleton key would not open Cyclops' door, so he kicked it in.

The apartment was empty.

Chapter Seven

Dennis Sachs seemed to be about forty years old. He was tall and deeply tanned, with massive shoulders and an athlete's easy stance. He opened the door of his room at the Hotel Capistan, and said, 'Detective Kling? Come in, won't you?'

'Thank you,' Kling said. He studied Sachs's face. The eyes were blue, with deep ridges radiating from the edges, starkly white against the bronzed skin. He had a large nose, an almost feminine mouth, a cleft chin. He needed a shave. His hair was brown.

The little girl, Anna, was sitting on a couch at the far end of the large living room. She had a doll across her lap, and she was watching television when Kling came in. She glanced up at him briefly, and then turned her attention back to the screen. A give-away program was in progress, the m.c. unveiling a huge motor launch to the delighted shrieks of the studio audience. The couch was upholstered in a lush green fabric against which the child's blonde hair shone lustrously. The place was oppressively over-furnished, undoubtedly part of a suite, with two doors leading from the living room to the adjoining bedrooms. A small cooking alcove was tucked discreetly into a corner near the entrance door, a screen drawn across it. The dominant colors of the suite were pale yellows and deep greens, the rugs were thick, the furniture was exquisitely carved. Kling suddenly wondered how much all this was costing Sachs per day, and then tried to remember where he'd picked up the notion that archaeologists were poverty-stricken.

'Sit down,' Sachs said. 'Can I get you a drink?'

'I'm on duty,' Kling said.

'Oh, sorry. Something soft then? A Coke? Seven-Up? I think we've got some in the refrigerator.'

'Thank you, no,' Kling said.

The men sat. From his wing chair, Kling could see

through the large windows and out over the park to where the skyscrapers lined the city. The sky behind the buildings was a vibrant blue. Sachs sat facing him, limned with the light flowing through the windows.

'The people at the Children's Shelter told me you got to the city late Monday, Mr Sachs. May I ask where in Arizona you were?'

'Well, part of the time I was in the desert, and the rest of the time I was staying in a little town called Rainfield, have you ever heard of it?'

'No.'

'Yes. Well, I'm not surprised,' Sachs said. 'It's on the edge of the desert. Just a single hotel, a depot, a general store, and that's it.'

'What were you doing in the desert?'

'We're on a dig, I thought you knew that. I'm part of an archaeological team headed by Dr Oliver Tarsmith. We're trying to trace the route of the Hohokam in Arizona.'

'The Hohokam?'

'Yes, that's a Pima Indian word meaning "those who have vanished." The Hohokam were a tribe once living in Arizona, haven't you ever heard of them?'

'No, I'm afraid I haven't.'

'Yes, well. In any case, they seem to have had their origins in Old Mexico. In fact, archaeologists like myself have found copper bells and other objects that definitely link the Hohokam to the Old Mexican civilization. And, of course, we've excavated ball courts—an especially large one at Snaketown—that are definitely Mexican or Mayan in origin. At one site, we found a rubber ball buried in a jar, and it's our belief that it must have been traded through tribes all the way from southern Mexico. That's where the wild rubber grows, you know.'

'No, I didn't know that.'

'Yes, well. The point is that we archaeologists don't know what route the Hohokam traveled from Mexico to Arizona and then to Snaketown. Dr Tarsmith's theory is that their point of entry was the desert just outside Rainfield. We are now excavating for archaeological evidence to support this theory.'

'I see. That sounds like interesting work.'

Sachs shrugged.

'Isn't it?'

'I suppose so.'

'You don't sound very enthusiastic.'

'Well, we haven't had too much luck so far. We've been out there for close to a year, and we've uncovered only the flimsiest sort of evidence, and . . . well, frankly, it's getting a bit tedious. We spend four days a week out on the desert, you see, and then come back into Rainfield late Thursday night. There's nothing much in Rainfield, and the nearest big town is a hundred miles from there. It can get pretty monotonous.'

'Why only *four* days in the desert?'

'Instead of five, do you mean? We usually spend Fridays making out our reports. There's a lot of paperwork involved, and it's easier to do at the hotel.'

'When did you learn of your wife's death, Mr Sachs?'

'Monday morning.'

'You had not been informed up to that time?'

'Well, as it turned out, a telegram was waiting for me in Rainfield. I guess it was delivered to the hotel on Saturday, but I wasn't there to take it.'

'Where were you?'

'In Phoenix.'

'What were you doing there?'

'Drinking, seeing some shows. You can get very sick of Rainfield, you know.'

'Did anyone go with you?'

'No.'

'How did you get to Phoenix?'

'By train.'

'Where did you stay in Phoenix?'

'At the Royal Sands.'

'From when to when?'

'Well, I left Rainfield late Thursday night. I asked Oliver—Dr Tarsmith—if he thought he'd need me on Friday, and he said he wouldn't. I guess he realized I was stretched a little thin. He's a very perceptive man that way.'

'I see. In effect, then, he gave you Friday off.'

'That's right.'

'No reports to write?'

'I took those with me to Phoenix. It's only a matter of organizing one's notes, typing them up, and so on.'

'Did you manage to get them done in Phoenix?'

'Yes, I did.'

'Now, Let me understand this, Mr Sachs . . .'

'Yes?'

'You left Rainfield sometime late Thursday night . . .'

'Yes, I caught the last train out.'

'What time did you arrive in Phoenix?'

'Sometime after midnight. I had called ahead to the Sands for a reservation.'

'I see. When did you leave Phoenix?'

'Mr Kling,' Sachs said suddenly, 'are you just making small talk, or is there some reason for your wanting to know all this?'

'I was simply curious, Mr Sachs. I know Homicide had sent a wire off to you, and I was wondering why you didn't receive it until Monday morning.'

'Oh. Well, I just explained that. I didn't get back to Rainfield until then.'

'You left Phoenix Monday morning?'

'Yes. I caught a train at about six a.m. I didn't want to miss the jeep.' Sachs paused. 'The expedition's jeep. We usually head out to the desert pretty early, to get some heavy work in before the sun gets too hot.'

'I see. But when you got back to the hotel, you found the telegram.'

'That's right.'

'What did you do then?'

'I immediately called the airport in Phoenix to find out what flights I could get back here.'

'And what did they tell you?'

'There was a TWA flight leaving at eight in the morning, which would get here at four-twenty in the afternoon—there's a two-hour time difference, you know.'

'Yes, I know that. Is that the flight you took?'

'No, I didn't. It was close to six-thirty when I called the airport. I might have been able to make it to Phoenix in time, but it would have been a very tight squeeze, and I'd have had to borrow a car. The trains out of Rainfield aren't that frequent, you see.'

'So what *did* you do?'

'Well, I caught American's eight-thirty flight, instead. Not a through flight; we made a stop at Chicago. I didn't get here until almost five o'clock that night.'

'That was Monday night?'

'Yes, that's right.'

'When did you pick up your daughter?'

'Yesterday morning. Today is Wednesday, isn't it?'

'Yes.'

'You lose track of time when you fly cross-country,' Sachs said.

'I suppose you do.'

The television m.c. was giving away a fourteen-cubic-foot refrigerator with a big, big one-hundred-and-sixty-pound freezer. The studio audience was applauding. Anna sat with her eyes fastened to the screen.

'Mr Sachs, I wonder if we could talk about your wife.'

'Yes, please.'

'The child . . .'

'I think she's absorbed in the program.' He glanced at her, and then said, 'Would you prefer we discussed it in one of the other rooms?'

'I thought that might be better, yes,' Kling said.

'Yes, you're right. Of course,' Sachs said. He rose and led Kling toward the larger bedroom. His valise, partially unpacked, was open on the stand alongside the bed. 'I'm afraid everything's a mess,' he said. 'It's been hurry up, hurry up from the moment I arrived.'

'I can imagine,' Kling said. He sat in an easy chair near the bed. Sachs sat on the edge of the bed and leaned over intently, waiting for him to begin. 'Mr Sachs, how long had you and your wife been divorced?'

'Three years. And we separated a year before that.'

'The child is how old?'

'Anna? She's five.'

'Is there another child?'

'No.'

'The way you said "Anna," I thought—'

'No, there's only the one child. Anna. That's all.'

'As I understand it, then, you and your wife separated the year after she was born.'

'That's right, yes. Actually, it was fourteen months. She was fourteen months old when we separated.'

'Why was that, Mr Sachs?'

'Why was what?'

'Why did you separate?'

'Well, you know.' Sachs shrugged.

'No, I don't.'

'Well, that's personal. I'm afraid.'

The room was very silent. Kling could hear the m.c. in the living room leading the audience in a round of applause for one of the contestants.

'I can understand that divorce is a personal matter, Mr Sachs, but—'

'Yes, it is.'

'Yes, I understand that.'

'I'd rather not discuss it, Mr Kling. Really, I'd rather not. I don't see how it would help you in solving . . . in solving my wife's murder. Really.'

'I'm afraid *I'll* have to decide what would help us, Mr Sachs.'

'We had a personal problem, let's leave it at that.'

'What sort of a personal problem?'

'I'd rather not say. We simply couldn't live together any longer, that's all.'

'Was there another man involved?'

'Certainly not!'

'Forgive me, but I think you can see how another man might be important in a murder case.'

'I'm sorry. Yes. Of course. Yes, it would be important. But it wasn't anything like that. There was no one else involved. There was simply a . . . a personal problem between the two of us and we . . . we couldn't find a way to resolve it, so . . . so we thought it best to split up. That's all there was to it.'

'What was the personal problem?'

'Nothing that would interest you.'

'Try me.'

'My wife is dead,' Sachs said.

'I know that.'

'Any problem she might have had is certainly—'

'Oh, it was *her* problem then, is that right? Not yours?'

'It was *our* problem,' Sachs said. 'Mr Kling, I'm not going to answer any other questions along these lines. If you insist that I do, you'll have to arrest me, and I'll get a lawyer, and we'll see about it. In the meantime, I'll just have to refuse to co-operate if that's the tack you're going to follow. I'm sorry.'

'All right, Mr Sachs, perhaps you can tell me whether or not you mutually agreed to the divorce.'

'Yes, we did.'

'Whose idea was it? Yours or hers?'

'Mine.'

'Why?'

'I can't answer that.'

'You know, of course, that adultery is the only grounds for divorce in this state.'

'Yes, I know that. There was no adultery involved. Tinka went to Nevada for the divorce.'

'Did you go with her?'

'No. She knew people in Nevada. She's from the West Coast originally. She was born in Los Angeles.'

'Did she take the child with her?'

'No. Anna stayed here with me while she was gone.'

'Have you kept in touch since the divorce, Mr Sachs?'

'Yes.'

'How?'

'Well, I see Anna, you know. We share the child. We agreed to that before the divorce. Stuck out in Arizona there, I didn't have much chance to see her this past year. But usually, I see quite a bit of her. And I talked to Tinka on the phone, I *used* to talk to her on the phone, and I also wrote to her. We kept in touch, yes.'

'Would you have described your relationship as a friendly one?'

'I loved her,' Sachs said flatly.

'I see.'

Again, the room was silent. Sachs turned his head away.

'Do you have any idea who might have killed her?' Kling asked.

'No.'

'None whatever?'

'None whatever.'

'When did you communicate with her last?'

'We wrote to each other almost every week.'

'Did she mention anything that was troubling her?'

'No.'

'Did she mention any of her friends who might have reason to . . . ?'

'No.'

'When did you write to her last?'

'Last week sometime.'

'Would you remember exactly when?'

'I think it was . . . the fifth or the sixth, I'm not sure.'

'Did you send the letter by air?'

'Yes.'

'Then it should have arrived here before her death.'

'Yes, I imagine it would have.'

'Did she usually save your letters?'

'I don't know. Why?'

'We couldn't find any of them in the apartment.'

'Then I guess she didn't save them.'

'Did *you* save *her* letters?'

'Yes.'

'Mr Sachs, would you know one of your wife's friends who answers this description: Six feet two or three inches tall, heavily built, in his late thirties or early forties, with straight blond hair and—'

'I don't know who Tinka saw after we were divorced. We led separate lives.'

'But you still loved her.'

'Yes.'

'Then why did you divorce her?' Kling asked again, and Sachs did not answer. 'Mr Sachs, this may be very important to us . . .'

'It isn't.'

'Was your wife a dyke?'

'No.'

'Are you a homosexual?'

'No.'

'Mr Sachs, *whatever* it was, believe me, it won't be something new to us. Believe me, Mr Sachs, and please trust me.'

'I'm sorry. It's none of your business. It has nothing to do with anything but Tinka and me.'

'Okay,' Kling said.

'I'm sorry.'

'Think about it. I know you're upset at the moment, but—'

'There's nothing to think about. There are some things I will never discuss with anyone, Mr Kling. I'm sorry, but I owe at least that much to Tinka's memory.'

'I understand,' Kling said, and rose. 'Thank you for your time. I'll leave my card, in case you remember anything that might be helpful to us.'

'All right,' Sachs said.

'When will you be going back to Arizona?'

'I'm not sure. There's so much to be arranged. Tinka's lawyer advised me to stay for a while, at least to the end of the month, until the estate can be settled, and plans made for Anna . . . there's so much to do.'

'*Is* there an estate?' Kling asked.

'Yes.'

'A sizable one?'

'I wouldn't imagine so.'

'I see.' Kling paused, seemed about to say something, and then abruptly extended his hand. 'Thank you again, Mr Sachs,' he said. 'I'll be in touch with you.'

Sachs saw him to the door. Anna, her doll in her lap, was still watching television when he went out.

At the squadroom, Kling sat down with a pencil and pad, and then made a call to the airport, requesting a list of all scheduled flights to and from Phoenix, Arizona. It took him twenty minutes to get all the information, and another ten minutes to type it up in chronological order. He pulled the single sheet from his machine and studied it:

AIRLINE SCHEDULES FROM PHOENIX AND RETURN

EASTBOUND:

Frequency	Airline & Flt.	Departing Phoenix	Arriving Here	Stops		
Exc. Sat.	American #946	12:25 AM	10:45 AM	(Tucson	12:57 AM-	1:35 AM
				(Chicago	6:35 AM-	8:00 AM
Daily	American # 93	7:25 AM	5:28 PM	(Tucson	7:57 AM-	8:25 AM
				(El Paso	9:10 AM-	9:40 AM
				(Dallas	12:00 PM-	12:30 PM
Daily	TWA #146	8:00 AM	4:20 PM	Chicago	12:58 PM-	1:30 PM
Daily	American # 68	8:30 PM	4:53 PM	Chicago	1:27 PM-	2:00 PM
Daily	American # 66	2:00 PM	10:23 PM	Chicago	6:57 PM-	7:30 PM

WESTBOUND:

Frequency	Airline & Flt.	Departing Here	Arriving Phoenix	Stops		
Exc. Sun.	American #965	8:00 AM	11:05 AM	Chicago	9:12 AM-	9:55 AM
Daily	TWA #147	8:30 AM	11:25 AM	Chicago	9:31 AM-	10:15 AM
Daily	American #981	4:00 PM	6:55 PM	Chicago	5:12 PM-	5:45 PM
Daily	TWA #143	4:30 PM	7:40 PM	Chicago	5:41 PM-	6:30 PM
Daily	American # 67	6:00 PM	10:10 PM	(Chicago	7:12 PM-	7:45 PM
				(Tucson	9:08 PM-	9:40 PM

It seemed entirely possible to him that Dennis Sachs could have taken either the twelve twenty-five flight from Phoenix late Thursday night, or any one of three flights early Friday morning, and still have been here in the city in time to arrive at Tinka's apartment by nine or nine-thirty p.m. He could certainly have killed his wife and caught an early flight back the next morning. Or any one of four flights on Sunday, all of which—because of the time difference—would have put him back in Phoenix that same night and in Rainfield by Monday to pick up the telegram waiting there for him. It was a possibility—remote, but a possibility nonetheless. The brown hair, of course, was a problem. Cyclops had said the man's hair was blond. But a commercial dye or bleach—

One thing at a time, King thought. Wearily, he pulled the telephone directory to him and began a methodical check of the two airlines flying to Phoenix. He told them he wanted to know if a man named Dennis Sachs, or any man with the initials D.S., had flown here from Phoenix last Thursday night or Friday morning, and whether or not he had made the return flight any time during the weekend. The airlines were helpful and patient. They checked their flight lists. Something we don't ordinarily do, sir, is this a case involving a missing per-

son? No, Kling said, this is a case involving a murder.
Oh, well in that case, sir, but we don't ordinarily do
this, sir, even for the police, our flight lists you see . . .
Yes, well I appreciate your help, Kling said.

Neither of the airlines had any record of either a
Dennis Sachs or a D.S. taking a trip from or to Phoenix
at any time before Monday, April 12th. American Airlines had him listed as a passenger on Flight 68, which
had left Phoenix at eight-thirty a.m. Monday morning,
and had arrived here at four-fifty-three p.m. that afternoon. American reported that Mr Sachs had not as yet
booked return passage.

Kling thanked American and hung up. There was still
the possibility that Sachs had flown here and back before
Monday, using an assumed name. But there was no way
of checking that—and the only man who could make
any sort of a positive identification had been missing
since Monday night.

The meeting took place in Lieutenant Byrnes's office
at five o'clock that afternoon. There were five detectives
present in addition to Byrnes himself. Miscolo had
brought in coffee for most of the men, but they sipped
at it only distractedly, listening intently to Byrnes as he
conducted the most unorthodox interrogation any of
them had ever attended.

'We're here to talk about Monday afternoon,' Byrnes
said. His tone was matter-of-fact, his face expressed no
emotion. 'I have the duty chart for Monday, April
twelfth, and it shows Kling, Meyer and Carella on from
eight to four, with Meyer catching. The relieving team is
listed as Hawes, Willis and Brown, with Brown catching.
Is that the way it was?'

The men nodded.

'What time did you get here, Cotton?'

Hawes, leaning against the lieutenant's filing cabinet,
the only one of the detectives drinking tea, looked up
and said, 'It must've been about five.'

'Was Steve still here?'

'No.'

'What about you, Hal?'

'I got here a little early, Pete,' Willis said. 'I had some calls to make.'

'What time?'

'Four-thirty.'

'Was Steve still here?'

'Yes.'

'Did you talk to him?'

'Yes.'

'What about?'

'He said he was going to a movie with Teddy that night.'

'Anything else?'

'That was about it.'

'I talked to him, too, Pete,' Brown said. He was the only Negro cop in the room. He was sitting in the wooden chair to the right of Byrnes's desk, a coffee container clasped in his huge hands.

'What'd he say to you, Art?'

'He told me he had to make a stop on the way home.'

'Did he say where?'

'No.'

'All right, now let's get this straight. Of the relieving team, only two of you saw him, and he said nothing about where he might have been headed. Is that right?'

'That's right,' Willis said.

'Were you in the office when he left, Meyer?'

'Yes. I was making out a report.'

'Did he say anything to you?'

'He said good night, and he made some joke about bucking for a promotion, you know, because I was hanging around after I'd been relieved.'

'What else?'

'Nothing.'

'Did he say anything to you at any time during the afternoon? About where he might be going later on?'

'Nothing.'

'How about you, Kling?'

'No, he didn't say anything to me, either.'

'Were you here when he left?'

'No.'

'Where were you?'

'I was on my way home.'

'What time did you leave?'

'About three o'clock.'

'Why so early?'

There was a silence in the room.

'Why so early?' Byrnes said again.

'We had a fight.'

'What about?'

'A personal matter.'

'The man is dead,' Byrnes said flatly. 'There are no personal matters any more.'

'He sent me back to the office because he didn't like the way I was behaving during an interview. I got sore.' Kling paused. 'That's what we argued about.'

'So you left here at three o'clock?'

'Yes.'

'Even though you were supposed to be working with Carella on the Tinka Sachs case, is that right?'

'Yes.'

'Did you know where he was going when he left here?'

'No, sir.'

'Did he mention anything about wanting to question anyone, or about wanting to see anyone again?'

'Only the elevator operator. He thought it would be a good idea to check him again.'

'What for?'

'To verify a time he'd given us.'

'Do you think that's where he went?'

'I don't know, sir.'

'Have you talked to this elevator operator?'

'No, sir, I can't locate him.'

'He's been missing since Monday night,' Meyer said. 'According to Bert's report, he was expecting a visit from a man who said he was Carella.'

'Is that right?' Byrnes asked.

'Yes,' Kling said. 'But I don't think it *was* Carella.'

'Why not?'

'It's all in my report, sir.'

'You've read this, Meyer?'

'Yes.'

'What's your impression?'

'I agree with Bert.'

Byrnes moved away from his desk. He walked to the window and stood with his hands clasped behind his back, looking at the street below. 'He found something, that's for sure,' he said, almost to himself. 'He found *something* or *somebody,* and he was killed for it.' He turned abruptly. 'And not a single goddamn one of you knows where he was going. Not even the man who was allegedly working this case with him.' He walked back to his desk. 'Kling, you stay. The rest of you can leave.'

The men shuffled out of the room. Kling stood uncomfortably before the lieutenant's desk. The lieutenant sat in his swivel chair, and turned it so that he was not looking directly at Kling. Kling did not know where he was looking. His eyes seemed unfocused.

'I guess you know that Steve Carella was a good friend of mine,' Byrnes said.

'Yes, sir.'

'A good friend,' Byrnes repeated. He paused for a moment, still looking off somewhere past Kling, his eyes unfocused, and then said, 'Why'd you let him go out alone, Kling?'

'I told you, sir. We had an argument.'

'So you left here at three o'clock, when you knew goddamn well you weren't going to be relieved until four-forty-five. Now what the hell do you call that, Kling?'

Kling did not answer.

'I'm kicking you off this goddamn squad,' Byrnes said. 'I should have done it long ago. I'm asking for your transfer, now get the hell out of here.'

Kling turned and started for the door.

'No, wait a minute,' Byrnes said. He turned directly to Kling now, and there was a terrible look on his face, as though he wanted to cry, but the tears were being checked by intense anger.

'I guess you know, Kling, that I don't have the power to suspend you, I guess you know that. The power rests with the commissioner and his deputies, and they're civilians. But a man can be suspended if he's violated the rules and regulations or if he's committed a crime. The way I look at it, Kling, you've done *both* those things. You violated the rules and regulations by leaving this squadroom and heading home when you were supposed to be on duty, and you committed a crime by allowing Carella to go out there alone and get killed.'

'Lieutenant, I—'

'If I could personally take away your gun and your shield, I'd do it, Kling, believe me. Unfortunately, I can't. But I'm going to call the Chief of Detectives the minute you leave this office. I'm going to tell him I'd like you suspended pending a complete investigation, and I'm going to ask that he recommend that to the commissioner. I'm going to *get* that suspension, Kling, if I have to go to the mayor for it. I'll get departmental charges filed, and a departmental trial, and I'll get you dismissed from the force. I'm *promising* you. Now get the hell out of my sight.'

Kling walked to the door silently, opened it, and stepped into the squadroom. He sat at his desk silently for several moments, staring into space. He heard the buzzer sound on Meyer's phone, heard Meyer lifting the instrument to his ear. 'Yeah?' Meyer said. 'Yeah, Pete. Right. Right. Okay, I'll tell him.' He heard Meyer putting the phone back onto its cradle. Meyer rose and came to his desk. 'That was the lieutenant,' he said. 'He wants me to take over the Tinka Sachs case.'

Chapter Eight

The message went out on the teletype at a little before ten Thursday morning:

MISSING PERSON WANTED FOR QUESTION-
ING CONNECTION HOMICIDE XXX ERNEST
MESSNER ALIAS CYCLOPS MESSNER XXX
WHITE MALE AGE 68 XXX HEIGHT 6 FEET
XXX WEIGHT 170 LBS XXX COMPLETELY BALD
XXX EYES BLUE LEFT EYE MISSING AND
COVERED BY PATCH XXXXX LAST SEEN
VICINITY 1117 GAINESBOROUGH AVENUE
RIVERHEAD MONDAY APRIL 12 TEN THIRTY

PM EST XXX CONTACT MISPERBUR OR DET/
2G MEYER MEYER EIGHT SEVEN SQUAD
XXXXXXXXX

A copy of the teletype was pulled off the squadroom machine by Detective Meyer Meyer who wondered why it had been necessary for the detective at the Missing Persons Bureau to insert the word 'completely' before the word 'bald'. Meyer, who was bald himself, suspected that the description was redundant, over-emphatic, and undoubtedly derogatory. It was his understanding that a bald person had no hair. None. Count them. None. Why, then, had the composer of this bulletin (Meyer visualized him as a bushy-headed man with thick black eyebrows, a black mustache and a full beard) insisted on inserting the word 'completely', if not to point a deriding finger at all hairless men everywhere? Indignantly, Meyer went to the squadroom dictionary, searched through balas, balata, Balaton, Balboa, balbriggan, and came to:

bald (bôld) adj. **1.** lacking hair on some part of the scalp: *a bald head or person.* **2.** destitute of some natural growth or covering: *a bald mountain.* **3.** bare; plain; unadorned: *a bald prose style.* **4.** open; undisguised: *a bald lie.* **5.** *Zool.* having white on the head: *bald eagle.*

Meyer closed the book, reluctantly admitting that whereas it was impossible to be a little pregnant, it was not equally impossible to be a little bald. The composer of the bulletin, bushy-haired bastard that he was, had been right in describing Cyclops as 'completely bald'. If ever Meyer turned up missing one day, they would describe him in exactly the same way. In the meantime, his trip to the dictionary had not been a total loss. He would hereafter look upon himself as a person who lacked hair on his scalp, a person destitute of some natural growth, bare, plain and unadorned, open and undisguised, having white on the head. Hereafter, he would be known zoologically as The Bald Eagle—Nemesis of All Evil, Protector of the Innocent, Scourge of the Underworld!

'Beware The Bald Eagle!' he said aloud, and Arthur Brown looked up from his desk in puzzlement. Happily, the telephone rang at that moment. Meyer picked it up and said, '87th Squad.'

'This is Sam Grossman at the lab. Who'm I talking to?'

'You're talking to The Bald Eagle,' Meyer said.

'Yeah?'

'Yeah.'

'Well, this is The Hairy Ape,' Grossman said. 'What's with you? Spring fever?'

'Sure, it's a beautiful day out,' Meyer said, looking through the window at the rain.

'Is Kling there? I've got something for him on this Tinka Sachs case.'

'I'm handling that one now,' Meyer said.

'Oh? Okay. You feel like doing a little work, or were you planning to fly up to your aerie?'

'Up *your* aerie, Mac,' Meyer said, and burst out laughing.

'Oh boy, I see I picked the wrong time to call,' Grossman said. 'Okay. Okay. When you've got a minute later, give me a ring, Okay? I'll—'

'The Bald Eagle *never* has a minute later,' Meyer said. 'What've you got for me?'

'This kitchen knife. The murder weapon. According to the tag, it was found just outside her bedroom door, guy probably dropped it on his way out.'

'Okay, what about it?'

'Not much. Only it matches a few other knives in the girl's kitchen, so it's reasonable to assume it belonged to her. What I'm saying is the killer didn't go up there with his own knife, if that's of any use to you.'

'He took the knife from a bunch of other knives in the kitchen, is that it?'

'No, I don't think so. I think the knife was in the bedroom.'

'What would a knife be doing in the bedroom?'

'I think the girl used it to slice some lemons.'

'Yeah?'

'Yeah. There was a pitcher of tea on the dresser. Two lemons, sliced in half, were floating in it. We found lemon-juice stains on the tray, as well as faint scratches left by the knife. We figure she carried the tea, the lemons, and the knife into the bedroom on that tray. Then she sliced the lemons and squeezed them into the tea.'

'Well, that seems like guesswork to me,' Meyer said.

'Not at all. Paul Blaney is doing the medical examination. He says he's found citric-acid stains on the girl's left hand, the hand she'd have held the lemons with while slicing with the right. We've checked, Meyer. She was right-handed.'

'Okay, so she was drinking tea before she got killed,' Meyer said.

'That's right. The glass was on the night table near her bed, covered with her prints.'

'Whose prints were covering the knife?'

'Nobody's,' Grossman said. 'Or I should say *everybody's*. A whole mess of them, all smeared.'

'What about her pocketbook? Kling's report said—'

'Same thing, not a good print on it anywhere. There was no money in it, you know. My guess is that the person who killed her also robbed her.'

'Mmm, yeah,' Meyer said. 'Is that all?'

'That's all. Disappointing, huh?'

'I hoped you might come up with something more.'

'I'm sorry.'

'Sure.'

Grossman was silent for a moment. Then he said, 'Meyer?'

'Yeah?'

'You think Carella's death is linked to this one?'

'I don't know,' Meyer said.

'I liked that fellow,' Grossman said, and hung up.

Harvey Sadler was Tinka Sachs's lawyer and the senior partner in the firm of Sadler, McIntyre and Brooks, with offices uptown on Fisher Street. Meyer arrived there at ten minutes to noon, and discovered that Sadler was just about to leave for the Y.M.C.A. Meyer told him he was there to find out whether or not Tinka Sachs had left a will, and Sadler said she had indeed. In fact, they could talk about it on the way to the Y, if Meyer wanted to join him. Meyer said he wanted to, and the two men went downstairs to catch a cab.

Sadler was forty-five years old, with a powerful build and craggy features. He told Meyer he had played offensive back for Dartmouth in 1940, just before he was drafted into the army. He kept in shape nowadays, he said, by playing handball at the Y two afternoons a week, Mondays and Thursdays. At least, he *tried* to keep in shape. Even handball twice a week could not completely compensate for the fact that he sat behind a desk eight hours a day.

Meyer immediately suspected a deliberate barb. He had become oversensitive about his weight several weeks back when he discovered what his fourteen-year-old son Alan meant by the nickname 'Old Crisco'. A bit of offduty detective work uncovered the information that 'Old Crisco' was merely high school jargon for 'Old Fat-inthe-Can', a disrespectful term of affection if ever he'd heard one. He would have clobbered the boy, naturally, just to show who was boss, had not his wife Sarah agreed with the little vontz. You *are* getting fat, she told Meyer; you should begin exercising at the police gym. Meyer, whose boyhood had consisted of a series of taunts and jibes from Gentiles in his neighborhood, never expected to be put down by vipers in his own bosom. He looked narrowly at Sadler now, a soldier in the enemy camp, and suddenly wondered if he was becoming a paranoid Jew. Worse yet, an *obese* paranoid Jew.

His reservations about Sadler and also about himself vanished the moment they entered the locker room of the Y.M.C.A., which smelled exactly like the locker room of the Y.M.H.A. Convinced that nothing in the world could eliminate suspicion and prejudice as effectively as the aroma of a men's locker room, swept by a joyous wave of camaraderie, Meyer leaned against the lockers while Sadler changed into his handball shorts, and listened to the details of Tinka's will.

'She leaves everything to her ex-husband,' Sadler said. 'That's the way she wanted it.'

'Nothing to her daughter?'

'Only if Dennis predeceased Tinka. In that case, a trust was set up for the child.'

'Did Dennis know this?' Meyer asked.

'I have no idea.'

'Was a copy of the will sent to him?'

'Not by me.'

'How many copies did you send Tinka?'

'Two. The original was kept in our office safe.'

'Did she *request* two copies?'

'No. But it's our general policy to send two copies of any will to the testator. Most people like to keep one at home for easy reference, and the other in a safe deposit box. At least, that's been our experience.'

'We went over Tinka's apartment pretty thoroughly, Mr Sadler. We didn't find a copy of any will.'

'Then perhaps she *did* send one to her ex-husband. That wouldn't have been at all unusual.'

'Why not?'

'Well, they're on very good terms, you know. And, after all, he *is* the only real beneficiary. I imagine Tinka would have wanted him to know.'

'Mmm,' Meyer said. 'How large an estate is it?'

'Well, there's the painting.'

'What do you mean?'

'The Chagall.'

'I still don't understand.'

'The Chagall painting. Tinka bought it many years ago, when she first began earning top money as a model. I suppose it's worth somewhere around fifty thousand dollars today.'

'That's a sizable amount.'

'Yes,' Sadler said. He was in his shorts now, and he was putting on his black gloves and exhibiting signs of wanting to get out on the court. Meyer ignored the signs.

'What about the rest of the estate?' he asked.

'That's it,' Sadler said.

'That's what?'

'The Chagall painting *is* the estate, or at least the substance of it. The rest consists of household furnishings, some pieces of jewelry, clothing, personal effects—none of them worth very much.'

'Let me get this straight, Mr. Sadler. It's my understanding that Tinka Sachs was earning somewhere in the vicinity of a hundred and fifty thousand dollars a year. Are you telling me that all she owned of value at her death was a Chagall painting valued at fifty thousand dollars?'

'That's right.'

'How do you explain that?'

'I don't know. I wasn't Tinka's financial advisor. I was only her lawyer.'

'As her lawyer, did you ask her to define her estate when she asked you to draw this will?'

'I did.'

'How did she define it?'

'Essentially as I did a moment ago.'

'When was this, Mr Sadler?'

'The will is dated March twenty-fourth.'

'March twenty-fourth? You mean just last month?'

'That's right.'

'Was there any specific reason for her wanting a will drawn at that time?'

'I have no idea.'

'I mean, was she worried about her health or anything?'

'She seemed in good health.'

'Did she seem frightened about anything? Did she seem to possess a foreknowledge of what was going to happen?'

'No, she did not. She seemed very tense, but not frightened.'

'Why was she tense?'

'I don't know.'

'Did you ask her about it?'

'No, I did not. She came to me to have a will drawn. I drew it.'

'Had you ever done any legal work for her prior to the will?'

'Yes. Tinka once owned a house in Mavis County. I handled the papers when she sold it.'

'When was that?'

'Last October.'

'How much did she get for the sale of the house?'

'Forty-two thousand, five hundred dollars.'

'Was there an existing mortage?'

'Yes. Fifteen thousand dollars went to pay it off. The remainder went to Tinka.'

'Twenty . . .' Meyer hesitated, calculating. 'Twenty-seven thousand, five hundred dollars went to Tinka, is that right?'

'Yes.'

'In cash?'

'Yes.'

'Where is it, Mr Sadler?'

'I asked her that when we were preparing the will. I was concerned about estate taxes, you know, and about who would inherit the money she had realized on the sale of the house. But she told me she had used it for personal needs.'

'She had spent it?'

'Yes.' Sadler paused. 'Mr Meyer, I only play here two afternoons a week, and I'm very jealous of my time. I was hoping . . .'

'I won't be much longer, please bear with me. I'm only trying to find out what Tinka did with all this money that came her way. According to you, she didn't have a penny of it when she died.'

'I'm only reporting what she told me. I listed her assets as she defined them for me.'

'Could I see a copy of the will, Mr Sadler?'

'Certainly. But it's in my safe at the office, and I won't be going back there today. If you'd like to come by in the morning . . .'

'I'd hoped to get a look at it before—'

'I assure you that I've faithfully reported everything in the will. As I told you, I was only her lawyer, not her financial adviser.'

'Did she *have* a financial adviser?'

'I don't know.'

'Mr Sadler, did you handle Tinka's divorce for her?'

'No. I began representing her only last year, when she sold the house. I didn't know her before then, and I don't know who handled the divorce.'

'One last question,' Meyer said. 'Is anyone else mentioned as a beneficiary in Tinka's will, other than Dennis or Anna Sachs?'

'They are the only beneficiaries,' Sadler said. 'And Anna only if her father predeceased Tinka.'

'Thank you,' Meyer said.

Back at the squadroom, Meyer checked over the typewritten list of all the personal belongings found in Tinka's apartment. There was no listing for either a will or a bankbook, but someone from Homicide had noted that a key to a safety deposit box had been found among the items on Tinka's workdesk. Meyer called Homicide to ask about the key, and they told him it had been turned over to the Office of the Clerk, and he could pick it up there if he was interested and if he was willing to sign a receipt for it. Meyer was indeed interested, so he went all the way downtown to the Office of the Clerk, where he searched through Tinka's effects, finding a tiny red snap-envelope with the safety deposit box key in it. The name of the bank was printed on the face of the miniature envelope. Meyer signed out the key and then —since he was in the vicinity of the various court buildings, anyway—obtained a court order authorizing him to open the safety deposit box. In the company of a court official, he went uptown again by subway and then ran through a pouring rain, courtesy of the vernal equinox, to the First Northern National Bank on the corner of Phillips and Third, a few blocks from where Tinka had lived.

A bank clerk removed the metal box from a tier of similar boxes, asked Meyer if he wished to examine the contents in private, and then led him and the court official to a small room containing a desk, a chair, and a chained ballpoint pen. Meyer opened the box.

There were two documents in the box. The first was a letter from an art dealer, giving appraisal of the Chagall painting. The letter stated simply that the painting had been examined, that it was undoubtedly a genuine Chagall, and that it could be sold at current market prices for anywhere between forty-five and fifty thousand dollars.

The second document was Tinka's will. It was stapled inside lawyer's blueback, the firm name Sadler, McIntyre and Brooks printed on the bottom of the binder, together with the address, 80 Fisher Street. Typewritten and centered on the page was the legend LAST WILL AND TESTAMENT OF TINKA SACHS. Meyer opened the will and began reading:

LAST WILL AND TESTAMENT
of
TINKA SACHS

I, Tinka Sachs, a resident of this city, county, and state, hereby revoke all wills and codicils by me at any time heretofore made and do hereby make, publish and declare this as and for my Last Will and Testament.

FIRST: I give, devise and bequeath to my former husband, DENNIS R. SACHS, if he shall survive me, and, if he shall not survive me, to my trustee, herein- after named, all of my property and all of my household and personal effects in- cluding without limitation, clothing, furniture and furnishings, books, jewelry, art objects, and paintings.

SECOND: If my former husband Dennis shall not survive me, I give, devise and bequeath my said estate to my Trustee hereinafter named, IN TRUST NEVERTHE- LESS, for the following uses and purposes:

(1) My Trustee shall hold, invest and re-invest the principal of said trust, and shall collect the income therefrom until my daughter, ANNA SACHS, shall attain the age of twenty-one (21) years, or sooner die.

(2) My Trustee shall, from time to time: distribute to my daughter ANNA be- fore she has attained the age of twenty-one (21) so much of the net income (and the net income of any year not so distrib- uted shall be accumulated and shall,

after the end of such year, be deemed principal for purposes of this trust) and so much of the principal of this trust as my Trustee may in his sole and unreviewable discretion determine for any purposes deemed advisable or convenient by said Trustee, provided, however, that no principal or income in excess of an aggregate amount of Five Thousand Dollars ($5,000) in any one year be used for the support of the child unless the death of the child's father, DENNIS R. SACHS, shall have left her financially unable to support herself. The decision of my Trustee with respect to the dates of distribution and the sums to be distributed shall be final.

(3) If my daughter, ANNA shall die before attaining the age of twenty-one (21) years, my Trustee shall pay over the then principal of the trust fund and any accumulated income to the issue of my daughter, ANNA, then living, in equal shares, and if there be no such issue then to those persons who would inherit from me had I died intestate immediately after the death of ANNA.

THIRD: I nominate, constitute and appoint my former husband, DENNIS R. SACHS, Executor of this my Last Will and Testament. If my said former husband shall predecease me or shall fail to qualify or cease to act as Executor, then I appoint my agent and friend, ARTHUR G. CUTLER, in his place as successor or substitute executor and, if my former husband shall predecease me, as TRUSTEES of the trust created hereby. If my said friend and agent shall fail to qualify or cease to act as Executor or Trustee, then I appoint his wife, LESLIE CUTLER, in his place as successor or substitute executor and/or trustee, as the case may be. Unless otherwise pro-

vided by law, no bond or other security
shall be required to permit any Executor
or Trustee to qualify or act in any
jurisdiction.

The rest of the will was boilerplate. Meyer scanned it
quickly, and then turned to the last page where Tinka
had signed her name below the words 'IN WITNESS
WHEREOF, I sign, seal, publish and declare this as my
Last Will and Testament' and where, below that, Harvey Sadler, William McIntyre and Nelson Brooks had
signed as attesting witnesses. The will was dated March
twenty-fourth.

The only thing Sadler had forgotten to mention—or
perhaps Meyer hadn't asked him about it—was that Art
Cutler had been named trustee in the event of Dennis
Sachs's death.

Meyer wondered if it meant anything.

And then he calculated how much money Tinka had
earned in eleven years at a hundred and fifty thousand
dollars a year, and wondered again why her only possession of any real value was the Chagall painting she had
drenched with blood on the night of her death.

Something stank.

Chapter Nine

He had checked and rechecked his own findings against
the laboratory's reports on the burned wreckage, and at
first only one thing seemed clear to Paul Blaney. Wher-
ever Steve Carella had been burned to death, it had not
been inside that automobile. The condition of the corpse
was unspeakably horrible; it made Blaney queasy just to
look at it. In his years as medical examiner, Blaney had
worked on cases of thermic trauma ranging from the
simplest burns to cases of serious and fatal exposure to
flame, light, and electric energy—but these were the
worst fourth-degree burns he had ever seen. The body
had undoubtedly been cooked for hours: The face was

unrecognizable, all of the features gone, the skin black and tight, the single remaining cornea opaque, the teeth undoubtedly loosened and then lost in the fire; the skin on the torso was brittle and split; the hair had been burned away, the flesh completely gone in many places, showing dark red-brown skeletal muscles and charred brittle bones. Blaney's internal examination revealed pale, cooked involuntary muscles, dull and shrunken viscera. Had the body been reduced to its present condition inside that car, the fire would have had to rage for hours. The lab's report indicated that the automobile, ignited by an explosion of gasoline, had burned with extreme intensity, but only briefly. It was Blaney's contention that the body had been burned elsewhere, and then put into the automobile to simulate death there by explosion and subsequent fire.

Blaney was not paid to speculate on criminal motivation, but he wondered now why someone had gone to all this trouble, especially when the car fire would undoubtedly have been hot enough to eliminate adequately and forever any intended victim. Being a methodical man, he continued to probe. His careful and prolonged investigation had nothing to do with the fact that the body belonged to a policeman, or even to a policeman he had known. The corpse on the table was not to him a person called Steve Carella; it was instead a pathological puzzle.

He did not solve that puzzle until late Friday afternoon.

Bert Kling was alone in the squadroom when the telephone rang. He lifted the receiver.

'Detective Kling, 87th Squad,' he said.

'Bert, this is Paul Blaney.'

'Hello, Paul, how are you?'

'Fine, thanks. Who's handling the Carella case?'

'Meyer's in charge. Why?'

'Can I talk to him?'

'Not here right now.'

'I think this is important,' Blaney said. 'Do you know where I can reach him?'

'I'm sorry, I don't know where he is.'

'If I give it to you, will you make sure he get it sometime tonight?'

'Sure,' Kling said.

'I've been doing the autopsy,' Blaney said. 'I'm sorry
I couldn't get back to you people sooner, but a lot of
things were bothering me about this, and I wanted to be
careful. I didn't want to make any statements that might
put you on the wrong track, do you follow?'

'Yes, sure,' Kling said.

'Well, if you're ready, I'd like to trace this for you
step by step. And I'd like to say at the onset that I'm absolutely convinced of what I'm about to say. I mean, I
know how important this is, and I wouldn't dare commit
myself on guesswork alone—not in a case of this na-
ture.'

'I've got a pencil,' Kling said. 'Go ahead.'

'To begin with, the comparative conditions of vehicle
and cadaver indicated to me that the body had been incinerated elsewhere for a prolonged period of time, and
only later removed to the automobile where it was
found. I now have further evidence from the lab to support this theory. I sent them some recovered fragments
of foreign materials that were embedded in the burned
flesh. The fragments proved to be tiny pieces of wood
charcoal. It seemes certain now that the body was consumed in a *wood* fire, and not a gasoline fire such as
would have occurred in the automobile. It's my opinion
that the victim was thrust headfirst into a fireplace.'

'What makes you think so?'

'The upper half of the body was severely burned,
whereas most of the pelvic region and all of the lower
extremities are virtually untouched. I think the upper
half of the body was pushed into the fireplace and kept
there for many hours, possibly throughout the night.
Moreover, I think the man was murdered *before* he was
thrown into the fire.'

'Before?'

'Yes, I examined the air passages for possible inhaled
soot, and the blood of carboxyhemoglobin. The presence of either would have indicated that the victim was
alive during the fire. I found neither.'

'Then how *was* he killed?' Kling asked.

'That would involve guesswork,' Blaney said. 'There's evidence of extradural hemorrhage, and there are also several fractures of the skull vault. But these may only be postmortem fractures resulting from charring, and I wouldn't feel safe in saying the victim was murdered by a blow to the head. Let's simply say he was dead before he was incinerated, and leave it at that.'

'Then why was he thrown into the fire?' Kling asked.

'To obliterate the body beyond recognition.'

'Go on.'

'The teeth, as you know, were missing from the head, making dental identification impossible. At first I thought the fire had loosened them, but upon further examination, I found bone fragments in the upper gum. I now firmly believe that the teeth were knocked out of the mouth before the body was incinerated, and I believe this was done to further prevent identification.'

'What are you saying, Blaney?'

'May I go on? I don't want any confusion about this later.'

'Please,' Kling said.

'There was no hair on the burned torso. Chest hair, underarm hair and even the upper region of pubic hair had been singed away by the fire. Neither was there any hair on the scalp, which would have been both reasonable and obvious had the body been thrust into a fireplace headfirst, as I surmise it was. But upon examination, I was able to find surviving hair roots in the subcutaneous fat below the dermis on the torso and arms, even though the shaft and epithelial sheath had been destroyed. In other words, though the fire had consumed whatever hair had once existed on the torso and arms, there was nonetheless evidence that hair *had been growing there.* I could find no such evidence on the victim's scalp.'

'What do you mean?'

'I mean that the man who was found in that automobile was bald to begin with.'

'What?'

'Yes, nor was this particularly surprising. The atrophied internal viscera, the distended aorta of the heart, the abundant fatty marrow, large medullary cavities, and dense compact osseous tissue all indicated a person well on in years. Moreover, it was my initial belief that only one eye had survived the extreme heat—the right eye—and that it had been rendered opaque whereas the left eye had been entirely consumed by the flames. I have now carefully examined that left socket and it is my conclusion that there had not been an eye in it for many many years. The optic nerve and tract simply do not exist, and there is scar tissue present which indicates removal of the eye long before—'

'Cyclops' Kling said. 'Oh my God, It's Cyclops!'
'Whoever it is,' Blaney said, 'it is *not* Steve Carella.'

He lay naked on the floor near the radiator.

He could hear rain lashing against the window panes, but the room was warm and he felt no discomfort. Yesterday, the girl had loosened the handcuff a bit, so that it no longer was clamped so tightly on his wrist. His nose was still swollen, but the throbbing pain was gone now, and the girl had washed his cuts and promised to shave him as soon as they were healed.

He was hungry.

He knew that the girl would come with food the moment it grew dark; she always did. There was one meal a day, always at dusk, and the girl brought it to him on a tray and then watched him while he ate, talking to him. Two days ago, she had showed him the newspapers, and he had read them with a peculiar feeling of unreality. The picture in the newspapers had been taken when he was still a patrolman. He looked very young and very innocent. The headline said he was dead.

He listened for the sound of her heels now. He could hear nothing in the other room; the apartment was silent. He wondered if she had gone, and felt a momentary pang. He glanced again at the waning light around the edges of the window shades. The rain drummed steadily against the glass. There was the sound of traffic below, tires hushed on rainswept streets. In the room, the gloom of dusk spread into the corners. Neon suddenly blinked against the drawn shades. He waited, listening, but there was no sound.

He must have dozed again. He was awakened by the

sound of the key being inserted in the door lock. He sat upright, his left hand extended behind him and mana-cled to the radiator, and watched as the girl came into the room. She was wearing a short silk dressing gown belted tightly at the waist. The grown was a bright red, and she wore black high-heeled pumps that added sever-al inches to her height. She closed the door behind her, and put the tray down just inside the door.

'Hello, doll,' she whispered.

She did not turn on the overhead light. She went to one of the windows instead and raised the shade. Green neon rainsnakes slithered along the glass pane. The floor was washed with melting green, and then the neon blinked out and the room was dark again. He could hear the girl's breathing. The sign outside flashed again. The girl stood near the window in the red gown, the green neon behind her limning her long legs. The sign went out.

'Are you hungry, doll?' she whispered, and walked to him swiftly and kissed him on the cheek. She laughed deep in her throat, then moved away from him and went to the door. The Llama rested on the tray alongside the coffeepot. A sandwich was on a paper plate to the right of the gun.

'Do I still need this?' she asked, hefting the gun and pointing it at him.

Carella did not answer.

'I guess not,' the girl said, and laughed again, that same low throaty laugh that was somehow not at all mirthful.

'Why am I alive?' he said. He was very hungry, and he could smell the coffee deep and strong in his nostrils, but he had learned not to ask for his food. He had asked for it last night, and the girl had deliberately postponed feeding him, talking to him for more than an hour be-fore she reluctantly brought the tray to him.

'You're not alive,' the girl said. 'You're dead. I showed you the papers, didn't I? You're dead.'

'Why didn't you really kill me?'

'You're too valuable.'

'How do you figure that?'

'You know who killed Tinka.'

'Then you're better off with me dead.'

'No.' The girl shook her head. 'No, doll. We want to know how you found out.'

'What difference does it make?'

'Oh, a lot of difference,' the girl said. 'He's very concerned about it, really he is. He's getting very impatient. He figures he made a mistake someplace, you see, and he wants to know what it was. Because if *you* found out, chances are somebody else will sooner or later. Unless you tell us what it was, you see. Then we can make sure nobody else finds out. Ever.'

'There's nothing to tell you.'

'There's plenty to tell,' the girl said. She smiled. 'You'll tell us. Are you hungry?'

'Yes.'

'Tch,' the girl said.

'Who was that in the burned car?'

'The elevator operator. Messner.' The girl smiled again. 'It was my idea. Two birds with one stone.'

'What do you mean?'

'Well, I thought it would be a good idea to get rid of Messner just in case he was the one who led you to us. Insurance. And I also figured that if everybody thought you were dead, that'd give us more time to work on you.'

'If Messner was my source, why do you have to work on me?'

'Well, there are a lot of unanswered questions,' the girl said. 'Gee, that coffee smells good, doesn't it?'

'Yes,' Carella said.

'Are you cold?'

'No.'

'I can get you a blanket if you're cold.'

'I'm fine, thanks.'

'I thought, with the rain, you might be a little chilly.'

'No.'

'You look good naked,' the girl said.

'Thank you.'

'I'll feed you, don't worry,' she said.

'I know you will.'

'But about those questions, they're really bothering him, you know. He's liable to get bugged completely and just decide the hell with the whole thing. I mean, I like having you and all, but I don't know if I'll be able to control him much longer. If you don't cooperate, I mean.'

'Messner was my source,' Carella said. 'He gave me the description.'

'Then it's a good thing we killed him, isn't it?'

'I suppose so.'

'Of course, that still doesn't answer those questions I was talking about.'

'What questions?'

'For example, how did you get the name? Messner may have given you a description, but where did you get the name? Or the address, for that matter?'

'They were in Tinka's address book. Both the name *and* the address.'

'Was the description there, too?'

'I don't know what you mean.'

'You know what I mean, doll. Unless Tinka had a *description* in that book of hers, how could you match a name to what Messner had told you?' Carella was silent. The girl smiled again. 'I'm *sure* she didn't have descriptions of people in her address book, did she?'

'No.'

'Good, I'm glad you're telling the truth. Because we found the address book in your pocket the night you came busting in here, and we know damn well there're no descriptions of people in it. You hungry?'

'Yes, I'm very hungry,' Carella said.

'I'll feed you, don't worry,' she said again. She paused. 'How'd you know the name and address?'

'Just luck. I was checking each and every name in the book. A process of elimination, that's all.'

'That's another lie,' the girl said. 'I wish you wouldn't lie to me.' She lifted the gun from the tray. She held the gun loosely in one hand, picked up the tray with the other, and then said, 'Back off.'

Carella moved as far back as the handcuff would allow. The girl walked to him, crouched, and put the tray on the floor.

'I'm not wearing anything under this robe,' she said.

'I can see that.'

'I thought you could,' the girl said, grinning, and then rose swiftly and backed toward the door. She sat in the chair and crossed her legs, the short robe riding up on her thighs. 'Go ahead,' she said, and indicated the tray with a wave of the gun.

Carella poured himself a cup of coffee. He took a quick swallow, and then picked up the sandwich and bit into it.

'Good?' the girl asked, watching.

'Yes.'

'I made it myself. You have to admit I take good care of you.'

'Sure,' Carella said.

'I'm going to take even better care of you,' she said. 'Why'd you lie to me? Do you think it's nice to lie to me?'

'I didn't lie.'

'You said you reached us by luck, a process of elimination. That means you didn't know who or what to expect when you got here, right? You were just looking for someone in Tinka's book who would fit Messner's description.'

'That's right.'

'Then why'd you kick the door in? Why'd you have a gun in your hand? See what I mean? You knew who he was *before* you got here. You knew he was the one. How?'

'I told you. It was just luck.'

'Ahh, gee, I wish you wouldn't lie. Are you finished there?'

'Not yet.'

'Let me know when.'

'All right.'

'I have things to do.'

'All right.'

'To *you*,' the girl said.

Carella chewed on the sandwich. He washed it down with a gulp of coffee. He did not look at the girl. She was jiggling her foot now, the gun hand resting in her lap.

'Are you afraid?' she asked.

'Of what?'

'Of what I might do to you.'

'No. Should I be?'

'I might break your nose all over again, who knows?'

'That's true, you might.'

'Or I might even keep my promise to knock out all your teeth.' The girl smiled. '*That* was my idea, too, you know, knocking out Messner's teeth. You people can make identifications from dental charts, can't you?'

'Yes.'

'That's what I thought. That's what I told him. *He* thought it was a good idea, too.'

'You're just *full* of good ideas.'

'Yeah, I have a lot of good ideas,' the girl said. 'You're not scared, huh?'

'No.'

'I would be, if I were you. Really, I would be.'

'The worst you can do is kill me,' Carella said. 'And since I'm already dead, what difference will it make?'

'I like a man with a sense of humor,' the girl said, but she did not smile. 'I can do worse than kill you.'

'What can you do?'

'I can corrupt you.'

'I'm incorruptible,' Carella said, and smiled.

'Nobody's incorruptible,' she said. 'I'm going to make you *beg* to tell us what you know. Really. I'm warning you.'

'I've told you everything I know.'

'Uh-uh,' the girl said, shaking her head. 'Are you finished there?'

'Yes.'

'Shove the tray away from you.'

Carella slid the tray across the floor. The girl went to it, stooped again, and picked it up. She walked back to the chair and sat. She crossed her legs. She began jiggling her foot.

'What's your wife's name?' she asked.

'Teddy.'

'That's a nice name. But you'll soon forget it soon enough.'

'I don't think so,' Carella said evenly.

'You'll forget her name, and you'll forget her, too.'

He shook his head.

'I promise,' the girl said. 'In a week's time, you won't even remember your *own* name.'

The room was silent. The girl sat quiet still except for the jiggling of her foot. The green neon splashed the floor, and then blinked out. There were seconds of darkness, and then the light came on again. She was standing now. She had left the gun on the seat of the chair and moved to the center of the room. The neon went out. When it flashed on again, she had moved closer to where he was manacled to the radiator.

'What would you like me to do to you?' she asked.

'Nothing.'

'What would you like to do to me?'

'Nothing,' he said.

'No?' she smiled. 'Look, doll.'

She loosened the sash at her waist. The robe parted over her breasts and naked belly. Neon washed the length of her body with green, and then blinked off. In the intermittent flashes, he saw the girl moving—as though in a silent movie—toward the light switch near the door, the open robe flapping loose around her. She snapped on the overhead light, and then walked slowly back to the center of the room and stood under the bulb. She held the front of her robe open, the long pale white sheath of her body exposed, the red silk covering her back and her arms, her fingernails tipped with red as glowing as the silk.

'What do you think?' she asked. Carella did not answer. 'You want some of it?'

'No,' he said.

'You're lying.'

'I'm telling you the absolute truth,' he said.

'I could make you forget her in a minute,' the girl said. 'I know things you never dreamed of. You want it?'

'No.'

'Just try and get it,' she said, and closed the robe and tightened the sash around her waist. 'I don't like it when you lie to me.'

'I'm not lying.'

'You're naked, mister, don't tell *me* you're not lying.'

She burst out laughing and walked to the door, opening

it, and then turned to face him again. Her voice was
very low, her face serious. 'Listen to me, doll,' she said.
You are *mine,* do you understand that? I can do whatever I want with you, don't you forget it. I'm promising
you right here and now that in a week's time you'll be
crawling on your hands and knees to me, you'll be licking my feet, you'll be *begging* for the opportunity to tell
me what you know. And once you tell me, I'm going to
throw you away, doll, I'm going to throw you broken
and cracked in the gutter, doll, and you're going to wish,
believe me, you are just going to *wish* it was you they
found dead in that car, believe me.' She paused. 'Think
about it,' she said, and turned out the light and went out
of the room.

He heard the key turning in the lock.

He was suddenly very frightened.

Chapter Ten

The car had been found at the bottom of a steep embankment off Route 407. The road was winding and
narrow, a rarely used branch connecting the towns of
Middlebarth and York, both of which were serviced by
wider, straighter highways. 407 was an oiled road, potholed and frost-heaved, used almost entirely by teenagers searching for a nighttime necking spot. The shoulders were muddy and soft, except for one place where
the road widened and ran into the approach to what had
once been a gravel pit. It was at the bottom of this pit
that the burned vehicle and its more seriously burned
passenger had been discovered.

There was only one house on Route 407, five and a
half miles from the gravel pit. The house was built of
native stone and timber, a rustic affair with a screened
back porch overlooking a lake reportedly containing
bass. The house was surrounded by white birch and flowering forsythia. Two dogwoods flanked the entrance
driveway, their buds ready to burst. The rain had
stopped but a fine mist hung over the lake, visible from

the turn in the driveway. A huge oak dripped clinging raindrops onto the ground. The countryside was still. The falling drops clattered noisily.

Detectives Hal Willis and Arthur Brown parked the car at the top of the driveway, and walked past the dripping oak to the front door of the house. The door was painted green with a huge brass doorknob centered in its lower panel and a brass knocker centered in the top panel. A locked padlock still hung in a hinge hasp and staple fastened to the door. But the hasp staple had been pried loose of the jamb, and there were deep gouges in the wood where a heavy tool had been used for the job. Willis opened the door, and they went into the house.

There was the smell of contained woodsmoke, and the stench of something else. Brown's face contorted. Gagging, he pulled a handkerchief from his back pocket and covered his nose and mouth. Willis had backed away toward the door again, turning his face to the outside air. Brown took a quick look at the large stone fireplace at the far end of the room, and then caught Willis by the elbow and led him outside.

'Any question in your mind?' Willis asked.

'None,' Brown said. 'That's the smell of burned flesh.'

'We got any masks in the car?'

'I don't know. Let's check the trunk.'

They walked back to the car. Willis took the keys from the ignition and leisurely unlocked the trunk. Brown began searching.

'Everything in here but the kitchen sink,' he said. 'What the hell's this thing?'

'That's mine,' Willis said.

'Well, what is it?'

'It's a hat, what do you think it is?'

'It doesn't look like any hat I've ever seen,' Brown said.

'I wore it on a plant couple of weeks ago.'

'What were you supposed to be?'

'A foreman.'

'Of what?'

'A chicken market.'

'That's *some* hat, man,' Brown said, and chuckled.

'That's a good hat,' Willis said. 'Don't make fun of

my hat. All the ladies who came in to buy chickens said it was a darling hat.'

'Oh, no question,' Brown said. 'It's a cunning hat.'

'Any masks in there?'

'Here's *one*. That's all I see.'

'The canister with it?'

'Yeah, it's all here.'

'Who's going in?' Willis said.

'I'll take it,' Brown said.

'Sure, and then I'll have the N.A.A.C.P. down on my head.'

'We'll just have to chance that,' Brown said, returning Willis's smile. 'We'll just have to chance it, Hal.' He pulled the mask out of its carrier, found the small tin of antidim compound, scooped some onto the provided cloth, and wiped it onto the eyepieces. He seated the facepiece on his chin, moved the canister and head harness into place with an upward, backward sweep of his hands, and then smoothed the edges of the mask around his face.

'Is if fogging?' Willis said.

'No, it's okay.'

Brown closed the outlet valve with two fingers and exhaled, clearing the mask. 'Okay,' he said, and began walking toward the house. He was a huge man, six feet four inches tall and weighing two hundred and twenty pounds, with enormous shoulders and chest, long arms, big hands. His skin was very dark, almost black, his hair was kinky and cut close to his scalp, his nostrils were large, his lips were thick. He looked like a Negro, which is what he was, take him or leave him. He did not at all resemble the white man's pretty concept of what a Negro *should* look like, the image touted in a new wave of magazine and television ads. He looked like himself. His wife Caroline liked the way he looked, and his daughter Connie liked the way he looked, and—more important —*he* liked the way he looked, although he didn't look so great at the moment with a mask covering his face and hoses running to the canister resting at the back of his neck. He walked into the house and paused just inside the door. There were parallel marks on the floor, beginning at the jamb and running vertically across the room.

He stooped to look at the marks more closely. They were black and evenly spaced, and he recognized them immediately as scuff marks. He rose and followed the marks to the fireplace, where they ended. He did not touch anything in or near the open mouth of the hearth; he would leave that for the lab boys. But he was convinced now that a man wearing shoes, if nothing else, had been dragged across the room from the door to the fireplace. According to what they'd learned yesterday, Ernest Messner had been incinerated in a wood-burning fire. Well, there had certainly been a wood-burning fire in this room, and the stink he and Willis had encountered when entering was sure as hell the stink of burned human flesh. And now there were heel marks leading from the door to the fireplace. Circumstantially, Brown needed nothing more.

The only question was whether the person cooked in this particular fireplace was Ernest Messner or somebody else.

He couldn't answer that one, and anyway his eye-pieces were beginning to fog. He went outside, took off the mask, and suggested to Willis that they drive into either Middlebarth or York to talk to some real estate agents about who owned the house with the smelly fireplace.

Elaine Hinds was a small, compact redhead with blue eyes and long fingernails. Her preference ran to small men, and she was charmed to distraction by Hal Willis, who was the shortest detective on the squad. She sat in a swivel chair behind her desk in the office of Hinds Real Estate in Middlebarth, and crossed her legs, and smiled, and accepted Willis's match to her cigarette, and graciously murmured, 'Thank you,' and then tried to remember what question he had just asked her. She uncrossed her legs, crossed them again, and then said, 'Yes, the house on 407.'

'Yes, do you know who owns it?' Willis asked. He was not unaware of the effect he seemed to be having on Miss Elaine Hinds, and he suspected he would never hear the end of it from Brown. But he was also a little puzzled. He had for many years been the victim of what he called the Mutt and Jeff phenomenon, a curious psychological and physiological reversal that made him irresistibly attractive to very big girls. He had never dated a girl who was shorter than five-nine in heels. One of his girl friends was five-eleven in her stockinged feet, and she was hopelessly in love with him. So he could not now understand why tiny little Elaine Hinds seemed so interested in a man who was only five feet eight inches tall, with the slight build of a dancer and the hands of a Black Jack dealer. He had, of course, served with the Marines and was an expert at judo, but Miss Hinds had no way of knowing that he was a giant among men, capable of breaking a man's back by the mere flick of an eyeball—well, almost. What then had caused her immediate attraction? Being a conscientious cop, he sincerely hoped it would not impede the progress of the investigation. In the meantime, he couldn't help noticing that she had very good legs and that she kept crossing and uncrossing them like an undecided virgin.

'The people who own that house,' she said, uncrossing her legs, 'are Mr and Mrs Jerome Brandt, would you like some coffee or something? I have some going in the other room.'

'No, thank you,' Willis said. 'How long have—'

'Mr Brown?'

'No, thank you.'

'How long have the Brandts been living there?'

'Well, they haven't. Not really.'

'I don't think I understand,' Willis said.

Elaine Hinds crossed her legs, and leaned close to Willis, as though about to reveal something terribly intimate. 'They bought it to use as a summer place,' she said. 'Mavis County is a marvelous resort area, you know, with many lakes and streams and with the ocean not too far from any point in the county. We're supposed to have less rainfall per annum than—'

'When did they buy it, Miss Hinds?'

'Last year. I expect they'll open the house after Memorial Day, but it's been closed all winter.'

'Which explains the broken hasp on the front door,' Brown said.

'Has it been broken?' Elaine said. 'Oh, dear,' and she uncrossed her legs.

'Miss Hinds, would you say that many people in the area knew the house was empty?'

'Yes, I'd say it was common knowledge, do you enjoy police work?'

'Yes, I do,' Willis said.

'It must be terribly exciting.'

'Sometimes the suspense is unbearable,' Brown said.

'I'll just *bet* it is,' Elaine said.

'It's my understanding,' Willis said, glancing sharply at Brown, 'that 407 is a pretty isolated road, and hardly ever used. Is that correct?'

'Oh, yes,' Elaine said. 'Route 126 is a much better connection between Middlebarth and York, and of course the new highway runs past both towns. As a matter of fact, most people in the area *avoid* 407. It's not a very good road, have you been on it?'

'Yes. Then, actually, anyone living around here would have known the house was empty, and would also have known the road going by it wasn't traveled too often. Would you say that?'

'Oh, yes, Mr Willis, I definitely *would* say that,' Elaine said.

Willis looked a little startled. He glanced at Brown, and then cleared his throat. 'Miss Hinds, what sort of people are the Brandts? Do you know them?'

'Yes, I sold the house to them. Jerry's an executive at IBM.'

'And his wife?'

'Maxine's a woman of about fifty, three or four years younger than Jerry. A lovely person.'

'Respectable people, would you say?'

'Oh, yes, *entirely* respectable,' Elaine said. 'My goodness, of *course* they are.'

'Would you know if either of them were up here Monday night?'

'I don't know. I imagine they would have called if they were coming. I keep the keys to the house here in the office, you see. I have to arrange for maintenance, and it's necessary—'

'But they didn't call to say they were coming up?'

'No, they didn't.' Elaine paused. 'Does this have anything to do with the auto wreck on 407?'

'Yes, Miss Hinds, it does.'

'Well, how could Jerry or Maxine be even *remotely* connected with that?'

'You don't think they could?'

'Of course not. I haven't seen them for quite some time now, but we did work closely together when I was handling the deal for them last October. Believe me, you couldn't find a sweeter couple. That's unusual, especially with people who have their kind of money.'

'Are they wealthy, would you say?'

'The house cost forty-two thousand five hundred dollars. They paid for it in cash.'

'Who'd they buy it from?' Willis asked.

'Well, you probably wouldn't know her, but I'll bet your wife would.'

'I'm not married,' Willis said.

'Oh? *Aren't* you?'

'Who'd they buy it from?' Brown asked.

'A fashion model named Tinka Sachs. Do you know her?'

If they had lacked, before this, proof positive that the man in the wrecked automobile was really Ernest Messner, they now possessed the single piece of information that tied together the series of happenings and eliminated the possibility of reasonable chance or coincidence:

1) Tinka Sachs had been murdered in an apartment on Stafford Place on Friday, April ninth.

2) Ernest Messner was the elevator operator on duty there the night of her murder.

3) Ernest Messner had taken a man up to her apartment and had later given a good description of him.

4) Ernest Messner had vanished on Monday night, April twelfth.

5) An incinerated body was found the next day in a wrecked auto on Route 407, the connecting road between Middlebarth and York, in Mavis County.

6) The medical examiner had stated his belief that the body in the automobile had been incinerated in a

wood fire elsewhere and only later placed in the automobile.

7) There was only one house on Route 407, five and a half miles from where the wrecked auto was found in the gravel pit.

8) There had been a recent wood fire in the fireplace of that house, and the premises smelled of burned flesh. There were also heel marks on the floor, indicating that someone had been dragged to the fireplace.

9) The house had once been owned by Tinka Sachs, and was sold only last October to its new owners.

It was now reasonable to assume that Tinka's murderer knew he had been identified, and had moved with frightening dispatch to remove the man who'd seen him. It was also reasonable to assume that Tinka's murderer knew of the empty house in Mavis County and had transported Messner's body there for the sole purpose of incinerating it beyond recognition, the further implication being that the murderer had known Tinka at least as far back as last October when she'd still owned the house. There were still a few unanswered questions, of course, but they were small things and nothing that would trouble any hard-working police force anywhere. The cops of the 87th wondered, for example, who had killed Tinka Sachs, and who had killed Ernest Messner, and who had taken Carella's shield and gun from him and wrecked his auto, and whether Carella was still alive, and where?

It's the small things in life that can get you down.

Those airline schedules kept bothering Kling.

He knew he had been taken off the case, but he could not stop thinking about those airline schedules, or the possibility that Dennis Sachs had flown from Phoenix and back sometime between Thursday night and Monday morning. From his apartment that night, he called Information and asked for the name and number of the hotel in Rainfield, Arizona. The local operator connected him with Phoenix Information, who said the only hotel listing they had in Rainfield was for the Major Powell on Main Street, was this the hotel Kling wanted? Kling said it was, and they asked if they should place the call. He knew that if he was eventually suspended, he would lose his gun, his shield and his salary until the case was decided, so he asked the operator how much the call would cost, and she said it would cost two dollars and ten cents for the first three minutes, and sixty-five cents for each additional minute. Kling told her to go ahead and place the call, station to station.

The man who answered the phone identified himself as Walter Blount, manager of the hotel.

'This is Detective Bert Kling,' Kling said. 'We've had a murder here, and I'd like to ask you some questions, if I may. I'm calling long distance.'

'Go right ahead, Mr Kling,' Blount said.

'To begin with, do you know Dennis Sachs?'

'Yes, I do. He's a guest here, part of Dr Tarsmith's expedition.'

'Were you on duty a week ago last Thursday night, April eighth?'

'I'm on duty *all* the time,' Blount said.

'Do you know what time Mr Sachs came in from the desert?'

'Well, I couldn't rightly say. They usually come in at about seven, eight o'clock, something like that.'

'Would you say they came in at about that time on April eighth?'

'I would say so, yes.'

'Did you see Mr Sachs leaving the hotel at any time that night?'

'Yes, he left, oh, ten-thirty or so, walked over to the railroad station.'

'Was he carrying a suitcase?'

'He was.'

'Did he mention where he was going?'

'The Royal Sands in Phoenix, I'd reckon. He asked us to make a reservation for him there, so I guess that's where he was going, don't you think?'

'Did you make the reservation for him personally, Mr Blount?'

'Yes, sir, I did. Single with a bath, Thursday night to Sunday morning. The rates—'

'What time did Mr Sachs return on Monday morning?'

'About six a.m. Had a telegram waiting for him here, his wife got killed. Well, I guess you know that, I guess that's what this is all about. He called the airport right away, and then got back on the train for Phoenix, hardly unpacked at all.'

'Mr Blount, Dennis Sachs told me that he spoke to his ex-wife on the telephone at least once a week. Would you know if that was true?'

'Oh, sure, he was always calling back east.'

'How often, would you say?'

'At least once a week, that's right. Even more than that, I'd say.'

'How much more?'

'Well . . . in the past two months or so, he'd call her three, maybe four times a week, something like that. He spent a hell of a lot of time making calls back east, ran up a pretty big phone bill here.'

'Calling his wife, you mean.'

'Well, not only her.'

'Who else?'

'I don't know who the other party was.'

'But he *did* make calls to other numbers here in the city?'

'Well, *one* other number.'

'Would you happen to know that number offhand, Mr Blount?'

'No, but I've got a record of it on our bills. It's not his wife's number because I've got that one memorized by heart, he's called it regular ever since he first came here a year ago. This other one is new to me.'

'When did he start calling it?'

'Back in February, I reckon.'

'How often?'

'Once a week, usually.'

'May I have the number, please?'

'Sure, just let me look it up for you.'

Kling waited. The line crackled. His hand on the receiver was sweating.

'Hello?' Blount said.

'Hello?'

'The number is SE— I think that stands for Sequoia —SE 3-1402.'

'Thank you,' Kling said.

'Not at all,' Blount answered.

Kling hung up, waited patiently for a moment with his hand on the receiver, lifted it again, heard the dial tone, and instantly dialed SE 3-1402. The phone rang insistently. He counted each separate ring, four, five, six, and suddenly there was an answering voice.

'Dr Levi's wire,' the woman said.

'This is Detective Kling of the 87th Squad here in the city,' Kling said. 'Is this an answering service?'

'Yes, sir, it is.'

'Whose phone did you say this was?'

'Dr Levi's.'

'And the first name?'

'Jason.'

'Do you know where I can reach him?'

'I'm sorry, sir, he's away for the weekend. He won't be back until Monday morning.' The woman paused. 'Is this in respect to a police matter, or are you calling for a medical appointment?'

'A police matter,' Kling said.

'Well, the doctor's office hours begin at ten Monday morning. If you'd care to call him then, I'm sure—'

'What's his home number?' Kling asked.

'Calling him there won't help you. He really is away for the weekend.'

'Do you know where?'

'No, I'm sorry.'

'Well, let me have his number, anyway,' Kling said.

'I'm not supposed to give out the doctor's home number. I'll try it for you, if you like. If the doctor's there —which I know he isn't—I'll ask him to call you back. May I have your number, please?'

'Yes, it's Roxbury 2, that's RO 2-7641.'

'Thank you.'

'Will you please call me in any event, to let me know if you reached him or not?'

'Yes, sir, I will.'

'Thank you.'

'What did you say your name was?'

'Kling, Detective Bert Kling.'

'Yes, sir, thank you,' she said, and hung up.

Kling waited by the phone.

In five minutes' time, the woman called back. She said she had tried the doctor's home number and—as she'd known would be the case all along—there was no answer. She gave him the doctor's office schedule and told him he could try again on Monday, and then she hung up.

It was going to be a long weekend.

Teddy Carella sat in the living room alone for a long while after Lieutenant Byrnes left, her hands folded in her lap, staring into shadows of the room and hearing nothing but the murmur of her own thoughts.

We now know, the lieutenant had said, that the man we found in the automobile definitely wasn't Steve. He's a man named Ernest Messner, and there is no question about it, Teddy, so I want you to know that. But I also want you to know this doesn't mean Steve is still alive. We just don't know anything about that yet, although we're working on it. The only thing it *does* indicate is that at least he's not for certain dead.

The lieutenant paused. She watched his face. He looked back at her curiously, wanting to be sure she understood everything he had told her. She nodded.

I knew this yesterday, the lieutenant said, but I wasn't sure, and I didn't want to raise your hopes until I had checked it out thoroughly. The medical examiner's office gave this top priority, Teddy. They still haven't finished the autopsy on the Sachs case because, well, you know, when we thought this was Steve, well, we put a lot of pressure on them. Anyway, it isn't. It isn't Steve, I mean. We've got Paul Blaney's word for that, and he's an excellent man, and we've also got the corroboration —what? Corroboration, did you get it? the corroboration of the chief medical examiner as well. So now I'm sure, so I'm telling you. And about the other, we're working on it, as you know, and as soon as we've got anything, I'll tell you that, too. So that's about all, Teddy. We're doing our best.

She had thanked him and offered him coffee, which he refused politely, he was expected home, he had to run, he hoped she would forgive him. She had shown him to the door, and then walked past the playroom, where Fanny was watching television, and then past the room where the twins were sound asleep and then into the living room. She turned out the lights and went to sit near the old piano Carella had bought in a secondhand store downtown, paying sixteen dollars for it and arranging to have it delivered by a furniture man in the precinct. He had always wanted to play the piano, he told her, and was going to start lessons—you're never too old to learn, right, sweetheart?

The lieutenant's news soared within her, but she was fearful of it, suspicious: Was it only a temporary gift that would be taken back? Should she tell the children, and then risk another reversal and a second revelation that their father was dead? 'What does that mean?' April had asked. 'Does dead mean he's never coming back?' And Mark had turned to his sister and angrily shouted, 'Shut up, you stupid dope!' and had run to his room where his mother could not see his tears.

They deserved hope.

They had the right to know there was hope.

She rose and went into the kitchen and scribbled a note on the telephone pad, and then tore off the sheet of paper and carried it out to Fanny. Fanny looked up when she approached, expecting more bad news, the lieutenant brought nothing but bad news nowadays. Teddy handed her the sheet of paper, and Fanny looked at it:

Wake the children.
Tell them their father
may still be alive.

Fanny looked up quickly.

'Thank God,' she whispered, and rushed out of the room.

Chapter Eleven

The patrolman came up to the squadroom on Monday morning, and waited outside the slatted rail divider until Meyer signaled him in. Then he opened the gate and walked over to Meyer's desk.

'I don't think you know me,' he said. 'I'm Patrolman Angieri.'

'I think I've seen you around,' Meyer said.

'I feel funny bringing this up because maybe you already know it. My wife said I should tell you, anyway.'

'What is it?'

'I only been here at this precinct for six months, this is my first percint, I'm a new cop.'

'Um-huh,' Meyer said.

'If you already know this, just skip it, okay? My wife says maybe you don't know it, and maybe it's important.'

'Well, what is it?' Meyer asked patiently.

'Carella.'

'What about Carella?'

'Like I told you, I'm new in the precinct, and I don't know all the detectives by name, but I recognized him later from his picture in the paper, though it was a picture from when he was a patrolman. Anyway, it was him.'

'What do you mean? I don't think I'm with you, Angieri.'

'Carrying the doll,' Angieri said.

'I still don't get you.'

'I was on duty in the hall, you know? Outside the apartment. I'm talking about the Tinka Sachs murder.'

Meyer leaned forward suddenly. 'Yeah, go ahead,' he said.

'Well, he come up there last Monday night, it must've been five-thirty, six o'clock, and he flashed the tin, and went inside the apartment. When he came out, he was in a hell of a hurry, and he was carrying a doll.'

'Are you telling me Carella was at the Sachs apartment last Monday night?'

'That's right.'

'Are you sure?'

'Positive.' Angieri paused. 'You *didn't* know this, huh? My wife was right.' He paused again. 'She's *always* right.'

'What did you say about a doll?'

'A doll, you know? Like kids play with? Girls? A big doll. With blonde hair, you know? A *doll*.'

'Carella came out of the apartment carrying a child's doll?'

'That's right.'

'Last Monday night?'

'That's right.'

'Did he say anything to you?'

'Nothing.'

'A doll,' Meyer said, puzzled.

It was nine a.m. when Meyer arrived at the Sachs apartment on Stafford Place. He spoke briefly to the superintendent of the building, a man named Manny Farber, and then took the elevator up to the fourth floor. There was no longer a patrolman on duty in the hallway. He went down the corridor and let himself into the apartment, using Tinka's own key, which had been lent to the investigating precinct by the Office of the Clerk.

The apartment was still.

He could tell at once that death had been here. There are different silences in an empty apartment, and if you are a working policeman, you do not scoff at poetic fallacy. An apartment vacated for the summer has a silence unlike that one that is empty only for the day, with its occupants expected back that night. And an apartment that has known the touch of death possesses a silence unique and readily identifiable to anyone who has ever stared down at a corpse. Meyer knew the silence of death, and understood it, though he could not have told you what accounted for it. The disconnected humless electrical appliances; the unused, undripping water taps; the unringing telephone; the stopped unticking clocks; the sealed windows shutting out all street noises; these were all a part of it, but they only contributed to the whole and were not its sum and substance. The real silence was something only felt, and had nothing to do with the absence of sound. It touched something deep within him the moment he stepped through the door. It seemed to be carried on the air itself, a shuddering reminder that death had passed this way, and that some of its frightening grandeur was still locked inside these rooms. He paused with his hand on the doorknob, and then sighed and closed the door behind him and went into the apartment.

Sunlight glanced through closed windows, dust beams silently hovered on the unmoving air. He walked softly, as though reluctant to stir whatever ghostly remnants still were here. When he passed the child's room, he looked through the open door and saw the dolls lined up in the bookcase beneath the windows, row upon row of dolls, each dressed differently, each staring back at him with unblinking glass eyes, pink cheeks glowing, mute red mouths frozen on the edge of articulation, painted lips parted over even plastic teeth, nylon hair in black, and red, and blonde, and the palest silver.

He was starting into the room when he heard a key turning in the front door.

The sound startled him. It cracked into the silent apartment like a crash of thunder. He heard the tumblers falling, the sudden click of the knob being turned. He moved into the child's room just as the front door opened. His eyes swept the room—bookcases, bed, closet, toy chest. He could hear heavy footsteps in the corridor, approaching the room. He threw open the closet door, drew his gun. The footsteps were closer. He eased the door toward him, leaving it open just a crack. Holding his breath, he waited in the darkness.

The man who came into the room was perhaps six feet two inches tall, with massive shoulders and a narrow waist. He paused just inside the doorway, as though sensing the presence of another person, seemed almost to be sniffing the air for a telltale scent. Then, visibly shrugging away his own correct intuition, he dismissed the idea and went quickly to the bookcases. He stopped in front of them and began lifting dolls from the shelves, seemingly at random, bundling them into his arms. He gathered up seven or eight of them, rose, turned toward the door, and was on his way out when Meyer kicked open the closet door.

The man turned, startled, his eyes opening wide. Foolishly, he clung to the dolls in his arms, first looking at Meyer's face, and then at the Colt .38 in Meyer's hand, and then up at Meyer's face again.

'Who are you?' he asked.

'Good question,' Meyer said. 'Put those dolls down, hurry up, on the bed there.'

'What . . .?'

'Do as I say, mister!'

The man walked to the bed. He wet his lips, looked at Meyer, frowned, and then dropped the dolls.

'Get over against the wall,' Meyer said.

'Listen, what the hell . . .?'

'Spread your legs, bend over, lean against the wall with your palms flat. Hurry up!'

'All right, take it easy.' The man leaned against the wall. Meyer quickly and carefully frisked him—chest, pockets, waist, the insides of his legs, Then he backed away from the man and said, 'Turn around, keep your hands up.'

The man turned, his hands high. He wet his lips again, and again looked at the gun in Meyer's hand.

'What are you doing here?' Meyer asked.

'What are *you* doing here?'

'I'm a police officer. Answer my—'

'Oh. Oh, okay,' the man said.

'What's okay about it?'

'I'm Dennis Sachs.'

'Who?'

'Dennis—'

'Tinka's husband?'

'Well, her ex-husband.'

'Where's your wallet?'

'Right here in my —'

'Don't reach for it! Bend over aginst that wall again, go ahead.'

The man did as Meyer ordered. Meyer felt for the wallet and found it in his right hip pocket. He opened it

to the driver's license. The name on the license was
Dennis Robert Sachs. Meyer handed it back to him.

'All right, put your hands down. What are you doing
here?'

'My daughter wanted some of her dolls,' Sachs said. 'I
came back to get them.'

'How'd you get in?'

'I have a key. I used to live here, you know.'

'It was my understanding you and your wife were divorced.'

'That's right.'

'And you still have a key?'

'Yes.'

'Did she know this?'

'Yes, of course.'

'And that's all you wanted here, huh? Just the dolls.'

'Yes.'

'Any doll in particular?'

'No.'

'Your daughter didn't specify any particular doll?'

'No, she simply said she'd like some of her dolls, and
she asked if I'd come get them for her.'

'How about *your* preference?'

'*My* preference?'

'Yes. Did *you* have any particular doll in mind?'

'Me?'

'That's right, Mr Sachs. You.'

'No. What do you mean? Are you talking about
dolls?'

'That's right, that's what I'm talking about.'

'Well, what would I want with any *specific* doll?'

'That's what *I'd* like to know.'

'I don't think I understand you.'

'Then forget it.'

Sachs frowned and glanced at the dolls on the bed.
He hesitated, then shrugged and said, 'Well, is it all right
to take them?'

'I'm afraid not.'

'Why not? They belong to my daughter.'

'We want to look them over, Mr Sachs.'

'For what?'

'I don't know for what. For *anything*.'

Sachs looked at the dolls again, and then he turned to Meyer and stared at him silently. 'I guess you know this has been a pretty bewildering conversation,' he said at last.

'Yeah, well, that's the way mysteries are,' Meyer answered. 'I've got work to do, Mr Sachs. If you have no further business here, I'd appreciate it if you left.'

Sachs nodded and said nothing. He looked at the dolls once again, and then walked out of the room, and down the corridor, and out of the apartment. Meyer waited, listening. The moment he heard the door close behind Sachs, he sprinted down the corridor, stopped just inside the door, counted swiftly to ten, and then eased the door open no more than an inch. Peering out into the hallway, he could see Sachs waiting for the elevator. He looked angry as hell. When the elevator did not arrive, he pushed at the button repeatedly and then began pacing. He glanced once at Tinka's supposedly closed door, and then turned back to the elevator again. When it finally arrived, he said to the operator, 'What took you so long?' and stepped into the car.

Meyer came out of the apartment immediately, closed the door behind him, and ran for the service steps. He took the steps down at a gallop, pausing only for an instant at the fire door leading to the lobby, and then opening the door a crack. He could see the elevator operator standing near the building's entrance, his arms folded across his chest. Meyer came out into the lobby quickly, glanced back once at the open elevator doors, and then ran past the elevator and into the street. He spotted Sachs turning the corner up the block, and broke into a run after him. He paused again before turning the corner. When he sidled around it, he saw Sachs getting into a taxi. There was no time for Meyer to go to his own parked car. He hailed another cab and said to the driver, just like a cop, 'Follow that taxi,' sourly reminding himself that he would have to turn in a chit for the fare, even though he knew Petty Cash would probably never reimburse him. The taxi driver turned for a quick look at Meyer, just to see who was pulling all this cloak and dagger nonsense, and then silently began following Sachs's cab.

'You a cop?' he asked at last.

'Yeah,' Meyer said.

'Who's that up ahead?'

'The Boston Strangler,' Meyer said.

'Yeah?'

'Would I kid you?'

'You going to pay for this ride, or is it like taking apples from a pushcart?'

'I'm going to pay for it,' Meyer said. 'Just don't lose him, okay?'

It was almost ten o'clock, and the streets were thronged with traffic. The lead taxi moved steadily uptown and then crosstown, with Meyer's driver skillfully following. The city was a bedlam of noise—honking horns, grinding gears, squealing tires, shouting drivers and pedestrians. Meyer leaned forward and kept his eye on the taxi ahead, oblivious to the sound around him.

'He's pulling up, I think,' the driver said.

'Good. Stop about six car lengths behind him.' The taxi meter read eighty-five cents. Meyer took a dollar bill from his wallet, and handed it to the driver the moment he pulled over to the curb. Sachs had already gotten out of this cab and was walking into an apartment building in the middle of the block.

'Is this all the city tips?' the driver asked. 'Fifteen cents on an eight-five-cent ride?'

'The city, my ass,' Meyer said, and leaped out of the cab. He ran up the street, and came into the building's entrance alcove just as the inner glass door closed behind Sachs. Meyer swung back his left arm and swiftly ran his hand over every bell in the row on the wall. Then, while waiting for an answering buzz, he put his face close to the glass door, shaded his eyes against the reflective glare, and peered inside. Sachs was nowhere in sight; the elevators were apparently around the corner of the lobby. A half-dozen answering buzzes sounded at once, releasing the lock mechanism on the door. Meyer pushed it open, and ran into the lobby. The floor indicator over the single elevator was moving, three, four, five —and stopped. Meyer nodded and walked out to the entrance alcove again, bending to look at the bells there. There were six apartments on the fifth floor. He was studying the names under the bells when a voice behind him said, 'I think you're looking for Dr Jason Levi.'

Meyer looked up, startled.

The man standing behind him was Bert Kling.

Dr Jason Levi's private office was painted an antiseptic white, and the only decoration on its walls was a large, easily readable calendar. His desk was functional and unadorned, made of grey steel, its top cluttered with medical journals and books, X-ray photographs, pharmaceutical samples, tongue depressors, prescription pads. There was a no-nonsense look about the doctor as well, the plain face topped with leonine white hair, the thick-lensed spectacles, the large cleaving nose, the thin-lipped mouth. He sat behind his desk and looked first at the detectives and then at Dennis Sachs, and waited for someone to speak.

'We want to know what you're doing here, Mr Sachs,' Meyer said.

'I'm a patient,' Sachs said.

'Is that true, Dr Levi?'

Levi hesitated. Then he shook his massive head. 'No,' he said. 'That is not true.'

'Shall we start again?' Meyer asked.

'I have nothing to say,' Sachs answered.

'Why'd you find it necessary to call Dr Levi from Arizona once a week?' Kling asked.

'Who said I did?'

'Mr Walter Blount, manager of the Major Powell Hotel in Rainfield.'

'He was lying.'

'Why would he lie?'

'I don't *know* why,' Sachs said. 'Go ask *him*.'

'No, we'll do it the easy way,' Kling said. 'Dr Levi, *did* Mr Sachs call you from Arizona once a week?'

'Yes,' Levi said.

'We seem to have a slight difference of opinion here,' Meyer said.

'Why'd he call you?' Kling asked.

'Don't answer that, Doctor!'

'Dennis, what are we trying to hide. She's dead.'

'You're a doctor, you don't have to tell them anything. You're like a priest. They can't force you to—'

'Dennis, she is dead.'

'Did your calls have something to do with your wife?' Kling asked.

'No,' Sachs said.

'Yes,' Levi said.

'Was *Tinka* your patient, Doctor, is that it?'

'Yes.'

'Dr Levi, I *forbid* you to tell these men anything more about—'

'She was my patient,' Levi said. 'I began treating her at the beginning of the year.'

'In January?'

'Yes. January fifth. More than three months ago.'

'Doctor, I swear on my dead wife that if you go ahead with this, I'm going to ask the A.M.A. to—'

'Nonsense!' Levi said fiercely. 'You wife is dead! If we can help them find her killer—'

'You're not helping them with anything! All you're doing is dragging her memory through the muck of a criminal investigation.'

'Mr Sachs,' Meyer said, 'whether you know it or not, her memory is already in the muck of a criminal investigation.'

'Why did she come to you, Doctor?' Kling asked. 'What was wrong with her?'

'She said she had made a New Year's resolution, said she had decided once and for all to seek medical assistance. It was quite pathetic, really. She was so helpless, and so beautiful, and so alone.'

'I *couldn't* stay with her any longer!' Sachs said. 'I'm not made of iron! I couldn't handle it. That's why we got the divorce. It wasn't my fault, what happened to her.'

'No one is blaming you for anything,' Levi said. 'Her illness went back a long time, long before she met you.'

'What was this illness, Doctor?' Meyer asked.

'Don't tell them!'

'Dennis, I *have* to—'

'You *don't* have to! Leave it the way it is. Let her

live in everyone's memory as a beautiful exciting woman instead of—'

Dennis cut himself off.

'Instead of what?' Meyer asked.

The room went silent.

'Instead of what?' he said again.

Levi sighed and shook his head.

'Instead of a drug addict.'

Chapter Twelve

In the silence of the squadroom later that day, they read Dr Jason Levi's casebook:

January 5

The patient's name is Tina Karin Sachs. She is divorced, has a daughter aged five. She lives in the city and leads an active professional life, which is one of the reasons she was reluctant to seek assistance before now. She stated, however, that she had made a New Year's resolution, and that she is determined to break the habit. She has been a narcotics user since the time she was seventeen, and is now addicted to heroin.

I explained to her that the methods of withdrawal which I had thus far found most satisfactory were those employing either morphine or methadone, both of which had proved to be adquate substitutes for whatever drugs or combinations of drugs my patients had previously been using. I told her, too, that I personally preferred the morphine method.

She asked if there would be much pain involved. Apparently she had once tried cold-turkey withdrawal and had found the attempt too painful to bear. I told her that she would experience withdrawal symptoms—nausea, vomiting, diarrhea, lacrimation, dilation of pupils, rhinorrhea, yawning, gooseflesh, sneezing, sweating—with either method. With morphine, the withdrawal would be more severe, but she could expect relative comfort after a week or so. With methadone, the withdrawal would be easier, but she might still feel somewhat tremulous for a long as a month afterward.

She said she wanted to think it over, and would call me when she had decided.

January 12

I had not expected to see or hear from Tinka Sachs again, but she arrived here today and asked my receptionist if I could spare ten minutes. I said I could, and she was shown into my private office, where we talked for more than forty-five minutes.

She said she had not yet decided what she should do, and wanted to discuss it further with me. She is, as she had previously explained, a fashion model. She receives top fees for her modeling and was now afraid that treatment might entail either pain or sickness which would cause her to lose employment, thereby endangering her career. I told her that her addiction to heroin had made her virtually careerless anyway, since she was spending much of her income on the purchase of drugs. She did not particularly enjoy this observation, and quickly rejoindered that she thoroughly relished all the fringe benefits of modeling—the fame, the recognition, and so on. I asked her if she really enjoyed anything but heroin, or really thought of anything but heroin, and she became greatly agitated and seemed about to leave the office.

Instead, she told me that I didn't know what it was like, and she hoped I understood she had been using narcotics since she was seventeen, when she'd first tried marijuana at a beach party in Malibu. She had continued smoking marijuana for almost a year, never tempted to try any of 'the real shit' until a photographer offered her a sniff of heroin shortly after she'd begun modeling. He also tried to rape her afterwards, a side effect that nearly caused her to abandon her beginning career as a model. Her near-rape, however, did not dissuade her from using marijuana or from sniffing heroin every now and then, until someone warned her that inhaling the drug could damage her nose. Since her nose was part of her face, and her face was part of what she hoped would become her fortune, she promptly stopped the sniffing process.

The first time she tried injecting the drug was with a confirmed addict, male, in a North Hollywood apartment. Unfortunately, the police broke in on them, and they were both arrested. She was nineteen years old at the time, and was luckily released with a suspended sentence. She came to this city the following month, determined never to fool with drugs again, hoping to put three thousand miles between herself and her former acquaintances. But she discovered, almost immediately upon arrival, that the drug was as readily obtainable here as it was in Los Angeles. Moreover, she began her association with the Cutler Agency several weeks after she got here, and found herself in possession of more money than she would ever need to support both herself *and* a narcotics habit. She began injecting the drug under her skin, into the soft tissue of her body. Shortly afterwards, she abandoned the subcutaneous route and began shooting heroin directly into her veins. She has been using it intravenously ever since, has for all intents and purposes been hopelessly hooked since she first began skin-popping. How, then, could I expect to cure her? How could she wake up each morning without knowing that a supply of narcotics was available, in fact accessible? I explained that hers was the common fear of all addicts about to undergo treatment, a reassurance she accepted without noticeable enthusiasm.

I think about it, she said again, and again left. I frankly do not believe she will ever return again.

January 20

Tinka Sachs began treatment today.

She has chosen the morphine method (even though she understands the symptoms will be more severe) because she does not want to endanger her career by a prolonged withdrawal, a curious concern for someone who has been endangering her career ever since it started. I had previously explained that I wanted to hospitalize her for several months, but she flatly refused hospitalization of any kind, and stated that the deal was off if that was part of the treatment. I told her that I could not guarantee lasting results unless she allowed me to hospitalize her, but she said we would have to hope for the best because she wasn't going to admit herself to any damn hospital. I finally extracted from her an agreement to stay at home under a nurse's care at least during the first several days of withdrawal, when the symptoms would be most severe. I warned her against making any illegal purchases and against associating with any known addicts or pushers. Our schedule is a rigid one. To start, she will receive ¼ grain of morphine four times daily —twenty minutes before each meal. The doses will be administered hypodermically, and the morphine will be dissolved in thiamine hydrocholoride.

It is my hope that withdrawal will be complete within two weeks.

                                                    January 21

I have prescribed Thorazine for Tinka's nausea, and belladonna and pectin for her diarrhea. The symptoms are severe. She could not sleep at all last night. I have instructed the nurse staying at her apartment to administer three grains of Nembutal tonight before Tinka retires, with further instructions to repeat 1½ grains if she does not sleep through the night.

Tinka has taken excellent care of her body, a factor on our side. She is quite beautiful and I have no doubt she is a superior model, though I am at a loss to explain how photographers can have missed her obvious addiction. How did she keep from 'nodding' before the cameras? She has scupulously avoided marking either her lower legs or her arms, but the insides of her thighs (she told me she does not model either lingerie or bathing suits) are covered with hit marks.

Morphine continues at ¼ grain four times daily.

                                                    January 22

I have reduced the morphine injections to ¼ grain twice daily, alternating with ⅛ grain twice daily. Symptoms are still severe. She has cancelled all of her sittings, telling the agency she is menstruating and suffering cramps, a complaint they have apparently heard from their models before. She shows no desire to eat. I have begun prescribing vitamins.

January 23

The symptoms are abating. We are now administering ⅛ grain four times daily.

January 24

Treatment continuing with ⅛ grain four times daily. The nurse will be discharged tomorrow, and Tinka will begin coming to my office for her injections, a procedure I am heartily against. But it is either that or losing her entirely, and I must go along.

January 25

Started one grain codeine twice daily, alternating with ⅛ grain morphine twice daily. Tinka came to my office at eight-thirty, before breakfast, for her first injection. She came again at twelve-thirty, and at six-thirty. I administered the last injection at her home at eleven-thirty. She seems exceptionally restless, and I have prescribed ½ grain of phenobarbital daily to combat this.

January 26

Tinka Sachs did not come to the office today. I called her apartment several times, but no one answered the telephone. I did not dare call the modeling agency lest they suspect she is undergoing treatment. At three o'clock, I spoke to her daughter's governess. She had just picked the child up at the play-school she attends. She said she did not know where Mrs Sachs was, and suggested that I try the agency. I called again at midnight. Tinka was still not home. The governess said I had awakened her. Apparently, she saw nothing unusual about her employer's absence. The working arrangement calls for her to meet the child after school and to spend as much time with her as is necessary. She said that Mrs Sachs is often gone the entire night, in which case she is supposed to take the child to school in the morning, and then call for her again at two-thirty. Mrs Sachs was once gone for three days, she said.

I am worried.

February 4

Tinka returned to the office again today, apologizing profusely, and explaining that she had been called out of town on an assignment; they were shooting some new tweed fashions and wanted a woodland background. I accused her of lying, and she finally admitted that she had not been out of town at all, but had instead spent the past week in the apartment of a friend from California. After further questioning, she conceded that her California friend is a drug addict, is in fact the man with whom she was arrested when she was nineteen years old. He arrived in the city last September, with very little money, and no place to live. She staked him for a while, and allowed him to live in her Mavis County house until she sold it in October. She then helped him to find an apartment on South Fourth, and she still sees him occasionally.

It was obvious that she had begun taking heroin again.

She expressed remorse, and said that she is more than ever determined to break the habit. When I asked if her friend expects to remain in the city, she said that he does, but that he has a companion with him, and no longer needs any old acquaintance to help him pursue his course of addiction.

I extracted a promise from Tinka that she would never see this man again, nor try to contact him.

We begin treatment again tomorrow morning. This time I insisted that a nurse remain with her for at least two weeks.

We will be starting from scratch.

February 9

We have made excellent progress in the past five days. The morphine injections have been reduced to ⅛ grain four times daily, and tomorrow we begin alternating with codeine.

Tinka talked about her relationship with her husband for the first time today, in connection with her resolve to break the habit. He is apparently an archaeologist working with an expedition somewhere in Arizona. She is in frequent touch with him, and in fact called him yesterday to say she had begun treatment and was hopeful of a cure. It is her desire, she said, to begin a new life with him once the withdrawal is complete. She knows he still loves her, knows that had it not been for her habit they would never have parted.

She said he did not learn of her addiction until almost a year after the child was born. This was all the more remarkable since the baby—fed during pregnancy by the bloodstream of her mother, metabolically dependent on heroin—was quite naturally an addict herself from the moment she was born. Dennis, and the family pediatrician as well, assumed she was a colicky baby, crying half the night through, vomiting, constantly fretting. Only Tinka knew that the infant was experiencing all the symptoms of cold-turkey withdrawal. She was tempted more than once to give the child a secret fix, but she refrained from doing so, and the baby survived the torment of force withdrawl only to face the subsequent storm of separation and divorce.

Tinka was able to explain the hypodermic needle Dennis found a month later by saying she was allergic to certain dyes in the nylon dresses she was modeling and that her doctor had prescribed an antihistamine in an attempt to reduce the allergic reaction. But she could not explain the large sums of money that seemed to be vanishing from their joint bank account, nor could she explain his ultimate discovery of three glassine bags of a white powder secreted at the back of her dresser drawer. She finally confessed that she was a drug addict, that she had been a drug addict for close to seven years and saw nothing wrong with it so long as she was capable of supporting the habit. He goddamn well knew she was earning most of the money in this household, anyway, so what the fuck did he want from her?

He cracked her across the face and told her they would go to see a doctor in the morning.

In the morning, Tinka was gone.

She did not return to the apartment until three weeks later, disheveled and bedraggled, at which time she told Dennis she had been on a party with three coloured musicians from a club downtown, all of them addicts. She could not remember what they had done together. Dennis had meanwhile consulted a doctor, and he told Tinka that drug addiction was by no means incurable, that there were ways of treating it, that success was almost certain if the patient—Don't make me laugh, Tinka said. I'm hooked through the bag and back, and what's more I like it, now what the hell do you think about that? Get off my back, you're worse than the monkey!

He asked for the divorce six months later.

During that time, he tried desperately to reach this person he had taken for a wife, this stranger, who was nonetheless the mother of his child, this driven animal whose entire life seemed bounded by the need for heroin. Their expenses were overwhelming. She could not let her career vanish because without her career she could hardly afford the enormous amounts of heroin she required. So she dressed the part of the famous model, and lived in a lavishly appointed apartment, and rode around town in hired limousines, and ate at the best restaurants, and was seen at all the important functions— while within her the clamour for heroin raged unabated. She worked slavishly, part of her income going toward maintaining the legend that was a necessary adjunct of her profession, the remainder going toward the purchase of drugs for herself and her friends.

There were always friends.

She would vanish for weeks at a time, lured by a keening song she alone heard, compelled to seek other addicts, craving the approval of people like herself, the comradeship of the dream society, the anonymity of the shooting gallery where scars were not stigmata and addiction was not a curse.

He would have left her sooner but the child presented a serious problem. He knew he could not trust Anna alone with her mother, but how could he take her with him on archaeological expeditions around the world? He realized that if Tinka's addiction were allowed to enter the divorce proceedings, he would be granted immediate custody of the child. But Tinka's career would automatically be ruined, and who knew what later untold hurt the attendant publicity could bring to Anna? He promised Tinka that he would not introduce the matter of her addiction if she would allow him to hire a responsible governess for the child. Tinka readily agreed. Except for her occasional binges, she considered herself to be a devoted and exemplary mother. If a governess would make Dennis happy and keep this sordid matter of addiction out of the proceedings, she was more than willing to go along with the idea. The arrangements were made.

Dennis, presumably in love with his wife, presumably concerned about his daughter's welfare, was nonetheless content to abandon one to eternal drug addiction, and the other to the vagaries and unpredictabilities of living with a confirmed junkie. Tinka, for her part, was glad to see him leave. He had become a puritanical goad, and she wondered why she'd ever married him in the first place. She supposed it had had something to do with the romantic notion of one day kicking the habit and starting a new life.

Which is what you're doing now, I told her.

Yes, she said, and her eyes were shining.

February 12

Tinka is no longer dependent on morphine, and we have reduced the codeine intake to one grain twice daily, alternating with ½ grain twice daily.

February 13

I received a long-distance call from Dennis Sachs today. He simply wanted to know how his wife was coming along and said that if I didn't mind he would call once a week—it would have to be either Friday or Saturday since he'd be in the desert the rest of the time—to check on her progress. I told him the prognosis was excellent, and I expressed the hope that withdrawal would be complete by the twentieth of the month.

February 14

Have reduced the codeine to ½ grain twice daily, and have introduced thiamine twice daily.

February 15

Last night, Tinka slipped out of the apartment while her nurse was dozing. She has not returned, and I do not know where she is.

February 20

Have been unable to locate Tinka.

March 1

Have called the apartment repeatedly. The governess continues to care for Anna—but there has been no word from Tinka.

March 8

In desperation, I called the Cutler Agency today to ask if they have any knowledge of Tinka's whereabouts. They asked me to identify myself, and I said I was a doctor treating her for a skin allergy (Tinka's own lie!). They said she had gone to the Virgin Islands on a modeling assignment and would not be back until the twentieth of March. I thanked them and hung up.

March 22

Tinka came back to my office today.

The assignment had come up suddenly, she said, and she had taken it, forgetting to tell me about it.

I told her I thought she was lying.

All right, she said. She had seized upon the opportunity as a way to get away from me and the treatment. She did not know why, but she had suddenly been filled with panic. She knew that in several days, a week at most, she would be off even the thiamine—and then what would there be? How could she possibly get through a day without a shot of *something*?

Art Cutler had called and proposed the St Thomas assignment, and the idea of sun and sand had appealed to her immensely. By coincidence, her friend from California called that same night, and when she told him where she was going he said that he'd pack a bag and meet her down there.

I asked her exactly what her connection is with this 'friend from California,' who now seems responsible for two lapses in her treatment. What lapse? she asked, and then swore she had not touched anything while she was away. This friend was simply *that*, a good friend.

But you told me he is an addict, I said.

Yes, he's an addict, she answered. But he didn't even

suggest drugs while we were away. As a matter of fact, I think I've kicked it completely. That's really the only reason I came here, to tell you that it's not necessary to continue treatment any longer. I haven't had anything, heroin or morphine or *anything*, all the while I was away. I'm cured.

You're lying, I said.

All right, she said. If I wanted the truth, it was her California friend who'd kept her out of prison those many years ago. He had told the arresting officers that he was a pusher, a noble and dangerous admission to make, and that he had forced a shot on Tinka. She had got off with the suspended sentence while he'd gone to prison; so naturally she was indebted to him. Besides, she saw no reason why she shouldn't spend some time with him on a modeling assignment, instead of running around with a lot of faggot designers and photographers, not to mention the Lesbian editor of the magazine. Who the hell did I think I was, her keeper?

I asked if this 'friend from California' had suddenly struck it rich.

What do you mean? she said.

Well, isn't it true that he was in need of money and a place to stay when he first came to the city?

Yes, that's true.

Then how can he afford to support a drug habit and also manage to take a vacation in the Virgin Islands? I asked.

She admitted that she paid for the trip. If the man had saved her from a prison sentence, what was so wrong about paying his fare and his hotel bill?

I would not let it go.

Finally, she told me the complete story. She had been sending him money over the years, not because he asked her for it, but simply because she felt she owed something to him. His lie had enabled her to come here and start a new life. The least she could do was send him a little money every now and then. Yes, she had been supporting him ever since he arrived here. Yes, yes, it was she who'd invited him along on the trip; there had been no coincidental phone call from him that night. Moreover, she had not only paid for *his* plane fare and hotel bill, but also for that of his companion, whom she described as 'an extremely lovely young woman'.

And no heroin all that while, right?

Tears, anger, defense.

Yes, there had been heroin! There had been enough heroin to sink the island, and she had paid for every drop of it. There had been heroin morning, noon, and night. It was amazing that she had been able to face the cameras at all, she had blamed her drowsiness on the sun. That needle had been stuck in her thigh constantly, like a glittering glass cock! Yes, there had been heroin, and she had loved every minute of it! What the hell did I want from her?

I want to cure you, I said.

March 23

She accused me today of trying to kill her. She said that I had been trying to kill her since the first day we met, that I know she is not strong enough to withstand the pains of withdrawal, and that the treatment will eventually result in her death.

Her lawyer has been preparing a will, she said, and she would sign it tomorrow. She would begin treatment after that, but she knew it would lead to her ultimate death.

I told her she was talking nonsense.

March 24

Tinka signed her will today.

She brought me a fragment of a poem she wrote last night:

> When I think of what I am
> And of what I might have been,
> I tremble.
> I fear the night.
> Throughout the day,
> I rush from dragons conjured in the dark.
> Why will they not

I asked her why she hadn't finished the poem. She said she couldn't finish it until she knew the outcome herself. What outcome do you want? I asked her.

I want to be cured, she said.
You *will* be cured, I told her.

March 25

We began treatment once more.

March 27

Dennis Sachs called from Arizona again to inquire about his wife. I told him she had suffered a relapse but that she had begun treatment anew, and that we were hoping for complete withdrawal by April 15th at the very latest. He asked if there was anything he could do for Tinka. I told him that the only person who could do anything for Tinka was Tinka.

March 28

Treatment continues.
¼ grain morphine twice daily.
⅛ grain morphine twice daily.

March 30

⅛ grain morphine four times daily.
Prognosis good.

March 31

⅛ grain morphine twice daily.
One grain codeine twice daily.

April 1

Tinka confessed today that she has begun buying heroin on the sly, smuggling it in, and has been taking it whenever the nurse isn't watching. I flew into a rage. She shouted 'April Fool!' and began laughing.
I think there is a chance this time.

April 2

One grain codeine four times daily.

April 3

One grain codeine twice daily.
½ grain codeine twice daily.

April 4

½ grain codeine four times daily.

April 5

½ grain codeine twice daily, thiamine twice daily.

April 6

Thiamine four times daily. Nurse was discharged to-day.

April 7

Thiamine three times daily.
We are going to make it!

April 8

Thiamine twice daily.

April 9

She told me today that she is certain the habit is almost kicked. This is my feeling as well. The weaning from hypodermics is virtually complete. There is only the promise of a new and rewarding life ahead.

That was where the doctor's casebook ended because that was when Tinka Sachs was murdered.

Meyer glanced up to see if Kling had finished the page. Kling nodded, and Meyer closed the book.

'He took two lives from her,' Meyer said. 'The one she was ending, and the one she was beginning.'

That afternoon Paul Blaney earned his salary for the second time in four days. He called to say he had completed the post-mortem examination of Tinka Sachs and had discovered a multitude of scars on both upper front thighs. It seemed positive that the scars had been caused by repeated intravenous injections, and it was Blaney's opinion that the dead girl had been a drug addict.

Chapter Thirteen

She had handcuffed both hands behind his back during one of his periods of unconsciousness, and then had used a leather belt to lash his feet together. He lay naked on the floor now and waited for her arrival, trying to tell himself he did not need her, and knowing that he needed her desperately.

It was very warm in the room, but he was shivering. His skin was beginning to itch but he could not scratch himself because his hands were manacled behind his back. He could smell his own body odors—he had not been bathed or shaved in three days—but he did not care about his smell or his beard, he only cared that she was not here yet, what was keeping her?

He lay in the darkness and tried not to count the minutes.

The girl was naked when she came into the room. She did not put on the light. There was the familiar tray in her hands, but it did not carry food any more. The Llama was on the left-hand side of the tray. Alongside the gun were a small cardboard box, a book of matches, a spoon with its handle bent back toward the bowl, and a glassine envelope.

'Hello, doll,' she said. 'Did you miss me?'

Carella did not answer.

'Have you meen waiting for me?' the girl asked. 'What's the matter, don't you feel like talking?' She laughed her mirthless laugh. 'Don't worry, baby,' she said. 'I'm going to fix you.'

She put the tray down on the chair near the door, and then walked to him.

'I think I'll play with you awhile,' she said. 'Would you like me to play with you?'

Carella did not answer.

'Well, if you're not even going to talk to me, I guess I'll just have to leave. After all, I know when I'm not—'

'No, don't go,' Carella said.

'Do you want me to stay?'

'Yes.'

'Say it.'

'I want you to stay.'

'That's better. What would you like, baby? Would you like me to play with you a little?'

'No.'

'Don't you like being played with?'

'No.'

'What do you like, baby?'

He did not answer.

'Well, you have to tell me,' she said, 'or I just won't give it to you.'

'I don't know,' he said.

'You don't know what you like?'

'Yes.'

'Do you like the way way I look without any clothes on?'

'Yes, you look all right.'

'But that doesn't interest you, does it?'

'No.'

'What *does* interest you?'

Again, he did not answer.

'Well, you *must* know what interests you. Don't you know?'

'No, I don't know.'

'Tch,' the girl said, and rose and began walking toward the door.

'Where are you going?' he asked quickly.

'Just to put some water in the spoon, doll,' she said soothingly. 'Don't worry. I'll be back.'

She took the spoon from the tray and walked out of the room, leaving the door open. He could hear the water tap running in the kitchen. Hurry up, he thought, and then thought, No, I don't need you, leave me alone, goddamn you, leave me alone!

'Here I am,' she said. She took the tray off the seat of the chair and then sat and picked up the glassine envelope. She emptied its contents into the spoon, and then struck a match and held it under the blackened bowl. 'Got to cook it up,' she said. 'Got to cook it up for my baby. You getting itchy for it, baby? Don't worry, I'll take care of you. What's your wife's name?'

'Teddy,' he said.

'Oh my,' she said, 'you still remember. That's a shame.' She blew out the match. She opened the small box on the tray, and removed the hypodermic syringe and needle from it. She affixed the needle to the syringe, and depressed the plunger to squeeze any air out of the cylindrical glass tube. From the same carboard box, which was the original container in which the syringe had been marketed, she took a piece of absorbent cotton, which she placed over the milky white liquid in the bowl of the spoon. Using the cotton as a filter, knowing that even the tiniest piece of solid matter would clog the tiny opening in the hypodermic needle, she drew the liquid up into the syringe, and then smiled and said, 'There we are, all ready for my doll.'

'I don't want it,' Carella said suddenly.

'Oh, honey, please don't lie to me,' she said calmly. 'I *know* you want it, what's your wife's name?'

'Teddy.'

'Teddy, tch, tch, well, well,' she said. From the cardboard box, she took a loop of string, and then walked to Carella and put the syringe on the floor beside him. She looped the piece of string around his arm, just above the elbow joint.

'What's your wife's name?' she asked.

'Teddy.'

'You want this, doll?'

'No.'

'Oooh, it's very good,' she said. 'We had some this afternoon, it was very good stuff. Aren't you just aching all over for it, what's your wife's name?'

'Teddy.'

'Has she got tits like mine?'

Carella did not answer.

'Oh, but that doesn't interest you, does it? All that intersts you is what's right here in this syringe, isn't that right?'

'No.'

'This is a very high-class shooting gallery, baby. No eyedroppers here, oh no. Everything veddy veddy hightone. Though I don't know how we're going to keep ourselves in junk now that little Sweetass is gone. He shouldn't have killed her, he really shouldn't have.'

'Then why did he?'

'I'll ask the questions, doll. Do you remember your wife's name?'

'Yes.'

'What is it?'

'Teddy.'

'Then I guess I'll go. I can make good use of this myself.' She picked up the syringe. 'Shall I go?'

'Do what you want to do.'

'If I leave this room,' the girl said, 'I won't come back until tomorrow morning. That'll be a long long night, baby. You think you can last the night without a fix?' She paused. 'Do you want this or not?'

'Leave me alone,' he said.

'No. No, no, we can't leave you alone. In a little while, baby, you are going to tell us everything you know, you are going to tell us exactly how you found us, you are going to tell us because if you don't we'll leave you here to drown in your own vomit. Now what's your wife's name?'

'Teddy.'

'No.'

'Yes. Her name is Teddy.'

'How can I give you this if your memory's so good?'

'Then don't give it to me.'

'Okay,' the girl said, and walked toward the door. 'Good-night, doll. I'll see you in the morning.'

'Wait.'

'Yes?' The girl turned. There was no expression on her face.

'You forgot your tourniquet,' Carella said.

'So I did,' the girl answered. She walked back to him and removed the string from his arm. 'Play it cool,' she said. 'Go ahead. See how far you get by playing it cool. Tomorrow morning you'll be rolling all over the floor when I come in.' She kissed him swiftly on the mouth. She sighed deeply. 'Ahh,' she said, 'why do you force me to be mean to you?'

She went back to the door and busied herself with putting the string and cotton back into the box, straightening the book of matches and the spoon, aligning the syringe with the other items.

'Well, good night,' she said, and walked out of the room, locking the door behind her.

Detective Sergeant Tony Kreisler of the Los Angeles Police Department did not return Meyer's call until nine o'clock that Monday night, which meant it was six o'clock on the Coast.

'You've had me busy all day long,' Kreisler said. 'It's tough to dig in the files for these ancient ones.'

'Did you come up with anything?' Meyer asked.

'I'll tell you the truth, if this hadn't been a homicide you're working on, I'd have given up long ago, said the hell with it.'

'What've you got for me?' Meyer asked patiently.

'This goes back twelve, thirteen years. You really think there's a connection?'

'It's all we've got to go on,' Meyer said. 'We figured it was worth a chance.'

'Besides, the city paid for the long-distance call, right?' Kreisler said, and began laughing.

'That's right,' Meyer said, and bided his time, and hoped that *Kreisler's* city was paying for *his* call, too.

Well, anyway,' Kreisler said, when his laughter had subsided, 'you were right about that arrest. We picked them up on a violation of Section 11500 of the Health and Safety Code. The girl's name wasn't Sachs then, we've got her listed as Tina Karin Grady, you suppose that's the same party?'

'Probably her maiden name,' Meyer said.

'That's what I figure. They were holed up in an apartment in North Hollywood with more than twenty-five caps of H, something better than an eighth of an ounce, not that it makes any difference out here. Out here, there's no minimum quantity constituting a violation. Any amount that can be analyzed as a narcotic is admissible in court. It's different with you guys, I know that.'

'That's right,' Meyer said.

'Anyway, the guy was a mainliner, hit marks all over his arms. The Grady girl looked like sweet young meat, it was tough to figure what she was doing with a creep like him. She claimed she didn't know he was an addict, claimed he'd invited her up to the apartment, got her drunk, and then forced a shot on her. There were no previous marks on her body, just that one hit mark in the crook of her el—'

'Wait a minute,' Meyer said.

'Yeah, what's the matter?'

'The *girl* claimed he'd forced the shot on her?'

'That's right. Said he got her drunk.'

'It wasn't the *man* who alibied her?'

'What do you mean?'

'Did the man claim he was a pusher and that he'd forced a fix on the girl?'

Kreisler began laughing again. 'Just catch a junkie who's willing to take a fall as a pusher. Are you kidding?'

'The girl told her doctor that the man alibied her.'

'Absolute lie,' Kreisler said. '*She* was the one who did all the talking, convinced the judge she was innocent, got off with a suspended sentence.'

'And the man?'

'Convicted, served his time at Soledad, minimum of two, maximum of ten.'

'Then *that's* why she kept sending him money. Not because she was indebted to him, but only because she felt guilty as hell.'

'She deserved a break,' Kreisler said. 'What the hell, she was a nineteen-year-old kid. How do you know? Maybe he *did* force a blast on her.'

'I doubt it. She'd been sniffing the stuff regularly and using pot since she was seventeen.'

'Yeah, well, we didn't know that.'

'What was the man's name?' Meyer asked.

'Fritz Schmidt.'

'Fritz? Is that a nickname?'

'No, that's his square handle. Fritz Schmidt.'

'What's the last you've got on him?'

'He was paroled in four. Parole Office gave him a clean bill of health, haven't had any trouble from him since.'

'Do you know if he's still in California?'

'Couldn't tell you.'

'Okay, thanks a lot,' Meyer said.

'Don't mention it,' Kreisler said, and hung up.

There were no listings for Fritz Schmidt in any of the city's telephone directories. But according to Dr Levi's casebook, Tinka's 'friend from California' had only arrived here in September. Hardly expecting any positive results, Meyer dialed the Information operator, identified himself as a working detective, and asked if she had anything for a Mr Fritz Schmidt in her new listings.

Two minutes later, Meyer and Kling clipped on their holsters and left the squadroom.

The girl came back into the room at nine-twenty-five. She was fully clothed. The Llama was in her right hand. She closed the door gently behind her, but did not bother to switch on the overhead light. She watched Carella silently for several moments, the neon blinking around the edges of the drawn shade across the room. Then she said, 'You're shivering, baby.'

Carella did not answer.

'How tall are you?' she asked.

'Six-two.'

'We'll get some clothes to fit you.'

'Why the sudden concern?' Carella asked. He was sweating profusely, and shivering at the same time, wanting to tear his hands free of the cuffs, wanting to kick out with his lashed feet, helpless to do either, feeling desperately ill and knowing the only thing that would cure him.

'No concern at all, baby,' she said. 'We're dressing you because we've got to take you away from here.'

'Where are you taking me?'

'Away.'

'Where?'

'Don't worry,' she said. 'We'll give you a nice big fix first.'

He felt suddenly exhilarated. He tried to keep the joy from showing on his face, tried not to smile, hoping against hope that she wasn't just teasing him again. He lay shivering on the floor, and the girl laughed and said, 'My, it's rough when a little jolt is overdue, isn't it?'

Carella said nothing.

'Do you know what an overdose of heroin is?' she asked suddenly.

The shivering stopped for just a moment, and then began again more violently. Her words seemed to echo in the room, do you know what an overdose of heroin is, overdose, heroin, do you, do you?

'Do you?' the girl persisted.

'Yes.'

'It won't hurt you,' she said. 'It'll *kill* you, but it won't hurt you.' She laughed again. 'Think of it, baby. How many addicts would you say there are in this city? Twenty thousand, twenty-one thousand, what's your guess?'

'I don't know,' Carella said.

'Let's make it twenty thousand, okay? I like round numbers. Twenty thousand junkies out there, all hustling around and wondering where their next shot is coming from, and here we are about to give you a fix that'd take care of seven or eight of them for a week. How about that? That's real generosity, baby.'

'Thanks,' Carella said. 'What do you think,' he started, and stopped because his teeth were chattering. He waited. He took a deep breath and tried again. 'What do you think you'll . . . you'll accomplish by killing me?'

'Silence,' the girl said.

'How?'

'You're the only one in the world who knows who we are or where we are. Once you're dead, silence.'

'No.'

'Ah, *yes*, baby.'

'I'm telling you no. They'll find you.'

'Uh-uh.'

'Yes.'

'How?'

'The same way I did.'

'Uh-uh. Impossible.'

'If *I* uncovered your mistake—'

'There *was* no mistake, baby.' The girl paused. 'There was only a little girl playing with her doll.'

The room was silent.

'We've got the doll, honey. We found it in your car, remember? It's a very nice doll. Very expensive, I'll bet.'

'It's a present for my daughter,' Carella said. 'I told you—'

'You weren't going to give your daughter a *used* doll for a present, were you? No, honey.' The girl smiled. 'I happened to look under the doll's dress a few minutes ago. Baby, it's all over for you, believe me.' She turned and opened the door. 'Fritz,' she yelled to the other room, 'come in here and give me a hand.'

The mailbox downstairs told them Fritz Schmidt was in apartment 34. They took the steps up two at a time, drawing their revolvers when they were on the third floor, and then scanning the numerals on each door as they moved down the corridor. Meyer put his ear to the door at the end of the hall. He could hear nothing. He moved away from the door, and then nodded to Kling. Kling stepped back several feet, bracing himself, his legs widespread. There was no wall opposite the end door, nothing to use as a launching support for a flat-footed kick at the latch. Meyer used Kling's body as the support he needed, raising his knee high as Kling shoved him out and forward. Meyer's foot connected. The lock sprang and the door swung wide. He followed it into the apartment, gun in hand, Kling not three feet behind him. They fanned out the moment they were inside the room. Kling to the right, Meyer to the left.

A man came running out of the room to the right of the large living room. He was a tall man with straight blond hair and huge shoulders. He looked at the detectives and then thrust one hand inside his jacket and down toward his belt. Neither Meyer nor Kling waited to find out what he was reaching for. They opened fire simultaneously. The bullets caught the man in his enormous chest and flung him back against the wall, which he clung to for just a moment before falling headlong to the floor. A second person appeared in the doorway. The second person was a girl, and she was very big, and she held a pistol in her right hand. A look of panic was riding her face, but it was curiously coupled with a fixed smile, as though she'd been expecting them all along and was ready for them, was in fact welcoming their arrival.

'Watch it, she's loaded!' Meyer yelled, but the girl swung around swiftly, pointing the gun into the other room instead, aiming it at the floor. In the split second it took her to turn and extend her arm, Kling saw the man lying trussed near the radiator. The man was turned away from the door, but Kling knew instinctively it was Carella.

He fired automatically and without hesitation, the first time he had ever shot a human being in the back, placing the shot high between the girl's shoulders. The Llama in her hand went off at almost the same instant, but the impact of Kling's slug sent her falling halfway across the room, her own bullet going wild. She struggled to rise as Kling ran into the room. She turned the gun on Carella again, but Kling's foot struck her extended hand, kicking the gun up as the second shot exploded. The girl would not let go. Her fingers were still tight around the stock of the gun. She swung it back a third time and shouted, 'Let me *kill* him, you bastard!' and tightened her finger on the trigger.

Kling fired again.

His bullet entered her forehead just above the right eye. The Llama went off as she fell backward, the bullet spanging against the metal of the radiator and then ricocheting across the room and tearing through the drawn window shade and shattering the glass behind it.

Meyer was at his side.

'Easy,' he said.

Kling had not cried since that time almost four years ago when Claire was killed, but he stood in the center of the neon-washed room now with the dead and bleeding girl against the wall and Carella naked and shivering near the radiator, and he allowed the hand holding the pistol to drop limply to his side, and then he began sobbing, deep bitter sobs that racked his body.

Meyer put his arm around Kling's shoulders.

'Easy,' he said again. 'It's all over.'

'The doll,' Carella whispered. 'Get the doll.'

Chapter Fourteen

The doll measured thirty inches from the top of her blonde head to the bottoms of her black patent-leather shoes. She wore white bobby sox, a ruffled white voile dress with a white nylon underslip, a black velveteen bodice, and a ruffled lace bib and collar. What appeared at first to be a simulated gold brooch was centered just below the collar.

The doll's trade name was Chatterbox.

There were two D-size flashlight batteries and one 9-volt transistor battery in a recess in the doll's plastic belly. The recess was covered with a flesh-colored plastic top that was kept in place by a simple plastic twist-lock. Immediately above the battery box there was a flesh-colored, oepn plastic grid that concealed the miniature electronic device in the doll's chest. It was this device after which the doll had been named by its creators. The device was a tiny recorder.

The brooch below the doll's collar was a knob that activated the recording mechanism. To record, a child simply turned the decorative knob counterclockwise, waited for a single beep signal, and began talking until the beep sounded again, at which time the knob had to be turned once more to its center position. In order to play back what had just been recorded, the child had only to turn the knob clockwise. The recorded message would continue to play back over and over again until the knob was once more returned to the center position.

When the detectives turned the brooch-knob clockwise, they heard three recorded voices. One of them belonged to Anna Sachs. It was clear and distinct because the doll had been in Anna's lap when she'd recorded her message on the night of her mother's murder. The message was one of reassurance. She kept saying over and over again to the doll lying across her lap, 'Don't be frightened, Chatterbox, please don't be frightened. It's nothing, Chatterbox, don't be frightened,' over and over again.

The second voice was less distinct because it had been recorded through the thin wall separating the child's bedroom from her mother's. Subsequent tests by the police laboratory showed the recording mechanism to be extremely sensitive for a device of its size, capable of picking up shouted words at a distance of twenty-five feet. Even so, the second voice would not have been picked up at all had Anna not been sitting very close to the thin dividing wall. And, of course, especially toward the end, the words next door had been screamed.

From beep to beep, the recording lasted only a minute and a half. Throughout the length of the recording, Anna talked reassuringly to her doll. "Don't be frightened, Chatterbox, please don't be frightened. It's nothing, Chatterbox, don't be frightened.' Behind the child's voice, a running counterpoint of horror, was the voice of Tinka Sachs, her mother. Her words were almost inaudible at first. They presented only a vague murmur of faraway terror, the sound of someone repeatedly moaning, the pitiable rise and fall of a voice imploring—but all without words because the sound had been muffled by the wall between the rooms. And then, as Tinka became more and more desperate, as her killer followed her unmercifully around the room with a knife blade, her voice became louder, the words became more distinct. 'Don't! Please don't!' always behind the child's soothing voice in the foreground, 'Don't be frightened, Chatterbox, please don't be frightened,' and her mother shrieking, 'Don't! Please don't! Please,' the voices intermingling, 'I'm bleeding, please, it's nothing, Chatterbox, don't be frightened, Fritz, stop, please, Fritz, stop, stop, oh please, it's nothing, Chatterbox, don't be frightened.'

The third voice sounded like a man's. It was nothing more than a rumble on the recording. Only once did a word come through clearly, and that was the word 'Slut!' interspersed between the child's reassurances to her doll, and Tinka's weakening cries for mercy.

In the end, Tinka shouted the man's name once again, 'Fritz!' and then her voice seemed to fade. The next word she uttered could have been a muted 'please', but it was indistinct and drowned out by Anna's 'Don't cry, Chatterbox, try not to cry.'

The detectives listened to the doll in silence, and then watched while the ambulance attendants carried Carella out on one stretcher and the still-breathing Schmidt out on another.

'The girl's dead,' the medical examiner said.

'I know,' Meyer answered.

'Who shot her?' one of the Homicide cops asked.

'I did,' Kling answered.

'I'll need the circumstances.'

'Stay with him,' Meyer said to Kling. 'I'll get to the hospital. Maybe that son of a bitch wants to make a statement before he dies.'

        I didn't intend to kill her.
        She was happy as hell when I came
in, laughing and joking because she
thought she was off the junk at last.

I told her she was crazy, she would never kick it.

I had not had a shot since three o'clock that afternoon, I was going out of my head. I told her I wanted money for a fix, and she said she couldn't give me money any more, she said she wanted nothing more to do with me or Pat, that's the name of the girl I'm living with. She had no right to hold out on me like that, not when I was so sick. She could see I was ready to climb the walls, so she sat there sipping her goddamn iced tea, and telling me she was not going to keep me supplied any more, she was not going to spend half her income keeping me in shit. I told her she owed it to me. I spent four years in Soledad because of her, the little bitch, she owed it to me! She told me to leave her alone. She told me to get out and leave her alone. She said she was finished with me and my kind. She said she had kicked it, did I understand, she had kicked it!

Am I going to die?

I

I picked

I picked the knife up from the tray.

I didn't intend to kill her, it was just I needed a fix, couldn't she see that? For Christ's sake, the times we used to have together. I stabbed her, I don't know how many times.

Am I going to die?

The painting fell off the wall, I remember that.

I took all the bills out of her pocketbook on the dresser, there was forty dollars in tens. I ran out of the bedroom and dropped the knife someplace in the hall, I guess, I don't even remember. I realized I couldn't take the elevator down, that much I knew, so I

went up to the roof and crossed over
to the next building and got down to the
street that way. I bought twenty caps
with the forty dollars. Pat and me got
very high afterwards, very high.

I didn't know Tina's kid was in the
apartment until tonight, when Pat
accidentally tipped to the goddamn talking doll.

If I'd known she was there, I might
have killed her, too. I don't know.

Fritz Schmidt never got to sign his dictated confession
because he died seven minutes after the police stenogra-
pher began typing it.

The lieutenant stood by while the two Homicide cops
questioned Kling. They had advised him not to make a
statement before Byrnes arrived, and now that he was
here they went about their routine task with dispatch.
Kling could not seem to stop crying. The two Homicide
cops were plainly embarrassed as they questioned him, a
grown man, a cop no less, crying that way. Byrnes
watched Kling's face, and said nothing.

The two Homicide copes were called Carpenter and
Calhoun. They looked very much alike. Byrnes had never met any Homicide cops who did not look exactly
alike. He supposed it was a trademark of their unique
specialty. Watching them, he found it difficult to remember who was Carpenter and who was Calhoun. Even
their voices sounded alike.

'Let's start with your name, rank, and shield number,'
Carpenter said.

'Bertram Kling, detective/third, 74579.'

'Squad?' Calhoun said.

'The Eight-Seven.' He was still sobbing. The tears
rolled down his face endlessly.

'Technically, you just committed a homicide, Kling.'

'It's excusable homicide,' Calhoun said.

'Justifiable,' Carpenter corrected.

'Excusable,' Calhoun repeated. 'Penal Law 1054.'

'Wrong,' Carpenter said. 'Justifiable, P.L. 1055.

Homicide is justifiable when committed by a public officer in arresting a person who has committed a felony and is fleeing from justice.' *Justifiable.*'

'Was the broad committing a felony?' Calhoun asked.

'Yes,' Kling said. He nodded. He tried to wipe the tears from his eyes. 'Yes. Yes, she was.' The tears would not stop.

'Explain it.'

'She was . . . she was ready to shoot Carella. She was trying to kill him.'

'Did you fire a warning shot?'

'No. Her back was turned to me and she was . . . she was leveling the gun at Carella, so I fired the minute I came into the room. I caught her between the shoulders, I think. With my first shot.'

'Then what?'

Kling wiped the back of his hand across his eyes. 'Then she . . . she started to fire again, and I kicked out at her hand, and the slug went wild. When she . . . when she got ready to fire the third time, I . . . I . . .'

'You killed her,' Carpenter said flatly.

'Justifiable,' Calhoun said.

'Absolutely,' Carpenter agreed.

'I said so all along,' Calhoun said.

'She'd already committed a felony by abducting a police officer, what the hell. And then she fired two shots at him. If that ain't a felony, I'll eat all the law books in this crumby state.'

'You got nothing to worry about.'

'Except the Grand Jury. This has to go to the Grand Jury, Kling, same as if you were an ordinary citizen.'

'You still got nothing to worry about,' Calhoun said.

'She was going to kill him,' Kling said blankly. His tears suddenly stopped. He stared at the two Homicide cops as though seeing them for the first time. 'Not again,' he said. 'I couldn't let it happen again.'

Neither Carpenter nor Calhoun knew what the hell Kling was talking about. Byrnes knew, but he didn't particularly feel like explaining. He simply went to Kling and said, 'Forget those department charges I mentioned. Go home and get some rest.'

The two Homicide cops didn't know what the hell *Byrnes* was talking about, either. They looked at each other, shrugged, and chalked it all up to the eccentricities of the 87th.

'Well,' Carpenter said. 'I guess that's that.'

'I guess that's that,' Calhoun said. Then, because Kling seemed to have finally gotten control of himself, he ventured a small joke. 'Stay out of jail, huh?' he said.

Neither Byrnes nor Kling even smiled.

Calhoun and Carpenter cleared their throats and walked out without saying good night.

She sat in the darkness of the hospital room and watched her sedated husband, waiting for him to open his eyes, barely able to believe that he was alive, praying now that he would be well again soon.

The doctors had promised to begin treatment at once. They had explained to her that it was difficult to fix the length of time necessary for anyone to become an addict, primarily because heroin procured illegally varied in its degree of adulteration. But Carella had told them he's received his first injection sometime late Friday night, which meant he had been on the drug for slightly more than three days. In their opinion, a person psychologically prepared for addiction could undoubtedly become a habitual user in that short a time, if he was using pure heroin of normal strength. But they were working on the assumption that Carella had never used drugs before and had been injected only with narcotics acquired illegally and therefore greatly adulterated. If this was the case, anywhere between two and three weeks would have been necessary to transform him into a confirmed addict. At any rate, they would begin withdrawal (if so strong a word was applicable at all) immediately, and they had no doubt that the cure (and again they apologized for using so strong a word) would be permanent. They had explained that there was none of the addict's usual psychological dependence evident in Carella's case, and then had gone on at great length about personality disturbances, and tolerance levels, and physical dependence—and then one of the doctors suddenly and quietly asked whether or not Carella had ever expressed a prior interest in experimenting with drugs.

Teddy had emphatically shaken her head.

Well, fine then, they said. We're sure everything will work out fine. We're confident of that, Mrs Carella. As for his nose, we'll have to make a more thorough examination in the morning. We don't know when he sustained the injury, you see, or whether or not the broken bones have already knitted. In any case, we should be able to reset it, though it may involve an operation. Please be assured we'll do everything in our power. Would you like to see him now?

She sat in the darkness.

When at last he opened his eyes, he seemed surprised to see her. He smiled and then said, 'Teddy'.

She returned the smile. She touched his face tentatively.

'Teddy,' he said again, and then—because the room was dark and because she would not see his mouth too clearly—he said something which she was sure she misunderstood.

'That's your name,' he said. 'I didn't forget.'